Here I Sit

René Fumoleau

Here I Sit

NOVALIS

Here I Sit
   is published by Novalis.

Cover design: Christiane Lemire, conceived from elements provided by
   René Fumoleau and Pierre Lapprand

Layout and design: Christiane Lemire, Francine Petitclerc

Photographs: René Fumoleau, unless otherwise indicated

© 1995 Novalis, Saint Paul University, Ottawa

Business Office: Novalis, 49 Front Street East, 2nd Floor, Toronto, Ontario
M5E 1B3. Editorial Office: Novalis, 223 Main Street, Ottawa,
Ontario   K1S 1C4.

Printed in Canada

Canadian Cataloguing in Publication Data

   Fumoleau, René

      Here I Sit

   Poems and short stories.
   ISBN 2-89088-734-0

      I. Title.

   PS8561.U8875H47   1995   C811'.54   C95-900907-8
   PR9199.3.F85H47   1995

NOVALIS

Table of Contents

9	Editor's Foreword
12	Preface
15	Breathing
16	Appearances
17	Artists all
18	Bills
19	Bingo
20	Fire
23	Believing
25	Fish and Sheep
26	Engineer
28	Back!
30	Home
31	Dene Church
33	Dene Christmas
35	Fort Freedom
37	Here I Sit
38	Birth Control
39	Catechism
40	Boxing
43	Jacket
48	Life
51	AIDS
53	Annunciation
55	Goats
57	Truck lights
58	Coca Cola
59	Texaco
61	Democracy
63	Forever
64	Divisions

66	Masks
67	Pretending
69	Be not afraid
72	On your way!
73	Margaret
75	Opinions
76	Such Potential
77	Serenity
78	Prayers
80	Bible
81	Priest
84	Lourdes
88	Can-Afford?
90	Full circle
92	Shampoo
94	Housing
96	Anything goes?
99	Birchbark Church
101	Bishop
103	Confession
104	Dear Father – A.D. 15
107	Dear Father – A.D. 30
109	Christian Unity
111	1903
113	Filipino Churches
115	Commitment
116	Family
118	Inconvenience
120	Land Claims
122	Mice
123	Needs
124	Engine
125	Beauty car
126	My love
127	Old age pension

129	Prayer
138	Photograph
141	Talents
143	Jennie
144	Yes, No
147	Ts'ąkui Theda
150	Self-Government
152	Pater Pauperum
153	Muskeg tea
155	Mirror
157	Awards night
159	Chocolate
160	Conformity
161	Click!
164	Experience
165	Counseling
167	Michael
168	Wait
169	Dene life
171	Carmelita
173	Children's Rights
175	Oranges
177	Marie and Charles
179	Cookie and Goldie
181	SAD
184	Insults
186	Mother
187	Up
188	Mountains
189	NATO
190	Embers
191	1975–1995

Editor's Foreword

by
Colin O'Connell

To read René Fumoleau is to be surprised.

Fumoleau's poetry works on us, like a cool northern wind, stripping us of our masks and the tiresome props of modern life. His poetry and stories don't add up to a neat little whole — a manageable bundle of worldly wisdom – but call us into an unpredictable world where the Spirit blows, where and when it wills. His narratives call us out and away as Abraham was called into the wilderness almost four millennia ago. We are invited on a Vision Quest.

Born in France in 1926, an Oblate of Mary Immaculate since 1946, ordained a priest in 1952, Fumoleau came to Denendeh (Northwest Territories) in 1953. He resided in Rádelį Kǫ́ę́ (Fort Good Hope) from 1953 to 1960, and from 1968 to 1969, and in Délįne (Fort Franklin) on Sahtú (Great Bear Lake) from 1960 to 1968. Since moving to Sǫmbak'è (Yellowknife) in 1970, he has been involved in a variety of ministries and pastoral activities. With the publication of *As Long as this Land Shall Last* in 1975, arguably the finest history of native treaties ever written in Canada, Fumoleau was launched on the national stage. This accomplishment was soon followed by his influential production of *I was Born Here* in 1976 (and its French version *Mon Pays est ma Vie* the following year) and *Dene Nation* in 1979, all critically acclaimed films. Some of the stories presented here have been widely published and a few acted on stage. The photo album *Denendeh* published in 1984 to celebrate the fifteenth anniversary of the Indian Brotherhood of the Northwest Territories, established Fumoleau as a photographer, too. Some of his photos are included in this book.

Readers of this collection will feel the force of the Oblate priest, but just as importantly, René, the man. His willingness to turn the light on himself and on the established church comes to the fore in poems such as *Priest*. There, with barely concealed irony, he reflects on the life of the "nice" priest saying his "nice" mass. In the poem *Catechism*, a teacher instructs the children in what Jesus said, but when the kids take it seriously and try to live the Gospel, parents complain and the teacher quickly relents: "I never told them to do it." We can hear the cock crowing for the third time.

Though often biting, the poet avoids easy sarcasm; his solidarity with others is far too strong. He takes to heart Saint Paul's injunction to pray unceasingly. Every word and every sigh is transformed and elevated in a dialogue with God. Or as Mohandas Gandhi, the great Hindu saint, once put it, "one can pray... not with the lips but the heart." Indeed some poems are eliptical fragments that draw us relentlessly towards that mystery that sustains all life.

Poetry and prayer merge.

Biblical echoes abound, too. In the poem *Embers*, the tiny flame that slowly becomes the crackling fire is reminiscent of Jesus's Parable of the Mustard Seed (Lk 13:19). Diminutive beginnings point the reader, if through a glass darkly, to the grandeur of the coming Kingdom. The fragile ember also echoes the Prologue of John where all believers are called to trust in the one true light who overcomes the darkness, but knows the darkness well. It's a light that burns in all traditions — as old as the fires of the first cave dwellers, as lasting as the Hanukkah flame, as joyous as the light in Hindu Dīvalī.

Readers will observe that Christ is rarely mentioned in Fumoleau's poems. But this doesn't mean that Christ isn't there. The poet reflects on "the God-shaped blank" in human experience where Christ's presence, often hidden, turns on the reader with sudden prophetic force. The crucified and risen One is there in the face of Leonard's mother who carefully tends for her dying son (*AIDS*), and also there in the words of Kochale whose celebration of life is a transcendent sign of aging with grace (*Here I Sit*). The whole of creation — finitude included — is accepted as being good.

Consider, too, the poem *Believing*. Rose Mary affirms her belief in beauty, in the dignity of each person, and in the triumph of love. But she also says that she doesn't believe in God. In an ironic pact with the reader, the poem implies that she still participates, if only unconsciously, in God's creation. Once again, the God-shaped blank. How else can one explain her *unconditional* sense of creation's beauty, her *unconditional* sense of human dignity, and her *unconditional* sense that love is indestructible.

For René Fumoleau, faith, it seems — even for those who profess not to believe — is nothing less than inevitable. The only question is "faith in what?" In this collection, self-discovery and discovery of God take place on the same path. And it's a path as wide as experience itself. Cosmic in scope, transcendent in depth, the author taps "the perennial tradition."

Indeed the author's irony and persistent questioning keep alive that sense of wonder that points beyond our finite life – our materiality and pride – to something far more durable. Nihilism just isn't enough anymore. Never, it seems, are we so aware of the reality of water as when we're thirsty – and never, perhaps, are we so aware of our need for mystery, as when we despair, consciously or otherwise, of achieving happiness through transient things.

It's here, I think, the poet's reflections on the Dene way of life, neatly juxtaposed to the White man's ways – but not in a caricatured or slavish way – drive that insight home. Dene culture reminds us that deeds are the litmus test of love, and that reticence of speech (because truth is fragile) is valued more than the loquacious spin of government officials. These are gifts that last.

I won't forget the pathos of the poem *Mother*, where the returning convict, afraid to speak to his aging mother after a fifteen-year absence, is finally set free from his mental shackles with his mother's simple request for a basin of warm water to wash her hair. "Talking it all out" has no place here.

Nor can I forget the gentle humour in *Pater Pauperum* where Frank says drily he'd prefer a "brother" to another episcopal "father." Also memorable is the poem *Housing,* in which a native displaced in squalid urban housing answers the question "is that where you live?" with the laconic remark: "No. That's where we die."

Fumoleau's poems, like the biblical parables, don't resolve issues so much as they leave us suspended by questions. That accounts for their ethical force.

Get ready to be snatched up by the winds of the Spirit.

Ottawa, Canada
April, 1995

11

Preface

"This is radio station TMAS (Tell Me a Story), and I am your host Bernie Hearne. Last week we broadcast four of René Fumoleau's stories. I had the opportunity to read a few more, and this morning, March 15, 1994, René is with me in the studio. Good morning, René, and let us start: Are your stories true stories?"

"Once a story is told or written, it is a true story."

"You know what I mean. Did your stories really happen?"

"Some stories did happen, and there was no reason to change a word. A few stories revealed themselves little by little. Some stories grew around a real event or conversation. Other stories travelled like light through a prism, and turned out colourful."

"But, René, do you write more from reality or from your feelings?"

"A story can grow out of mine or other people's feelings, feelings which find words for themselves. I may write a story to help myself understand a situation better. A story may also change according to the inspiration of the moment and thus become a new story."

"When did you start to write stories?"

"Very few stories before 1988. That year, I felt that buying Christmas cards and zipping them out was senseless. For me, a commercial card has less meaning than three coloured lines drawn by a friend on a piece of paper. So instead of mailing Christmas cards, I sent the story 'Planning Christmas.' Before Christmas 1989, I discovered Jesus' letter to his Father. I enjoyed those stories so much that I started to write about other topics and events."

"In your stories, you mention a number of people by name. Are those real names of real people?"

"Some names, as you say, are names of real people. I also changed and made up names to protect the anonymity of people."

"Do your stories have clear meanings? Do they carry a message?"

"Many stories have a clear message, at least for me, but a listener or a reader may wonder: 'What the heck does it mean?' I feel happy when someone says: 'The meaning of that story is very clear', and goes on explaining what I had never discovered myself. It is a sign of a good story."

"Are some of your stories connected to others? How should they be read?"

"Different people will read them differently. Donna, a friend, told me: 'I like the stories you lent me. I read them all in half an hour.' Kate, another friend, said: 'I glanced over two or three stories, but then the next one stirred something in me, and I thought about it for days.'"

"So, does it mean that your stories can happen also to other people?"

"Usually, stories are universal stories. I believe that anybody can read or listen to anyone of my stories, and feel: 'Oh yes, that happened to me also.... I heard that before.' Probably with different words or situations, but truly alike."

"René, are you going to publish a book of your stories some day? People may be interested."

"It's possible. My stories celebrate my own life. Yes, if my stories could help other people to learn and celebrate from their own experience."

"We all need to learn from each others, otherwise the world will never change and improve."

"Who would buy a book of my stories? Only people who can read and who are rich enough to buy books."

"Some poor people could benefit too."

"The poor, the unschooled, and the oppressed don't have enough money for food, much less for books. They are the people who will change the world, and they don't need to learn from books."

"Wow! René, your stories are leading us to a different level of discussion. A whole new topic, possibly for another interview, because we're running out of time. René, thank you for sharing your ideas and your feelings with us."

"Thank you, Bernie. I enjoyed your interview. I may even turn it into a story."

René Fumoleau

Breathing

"I have all that I want,
I have a huge mansion,
I have original artwork,
I have the finest food,
I have servants and maids,
I have three racing cars,
I have designer clothes,
I have fat bank accounts,
I have no happiness.
    What can I do?"

"You know the solution.
What's the very first thing
    you learned at your birth?"

"I don't know. Tell me."

"Oh yes, you know.
Everyone
    has to breathe in,
    and to breathe out."

Appearances

I flew to Ottawa for a meeting
    and I checked in at St. Paul University.

As I entered the elevator with my suitcase
    a woman asked me:

      "Are you a bishop?"

      "No, I am not."

I dropped my suitcase in my room,
    and, dressed as I was, I walked two blocks
    to a small self-service restaurant.

As I looked around, wondering how to proceed,
    a man asked me:

      "Are you the cook's helper here?"

      "No, I am not."

Artists all

In October 1991,
    I exhibited forty two of my photographs
    in a Montreal community centre.
Many visitors admired the portraits of young and old Dene,
    and the sceneries unique to their country.

An artist famous in Quebec and in Europe
    walked quietly back and forth around the room,
    trying to discover the mystery of each photograph.
He stood in front of the last photograph on the left.
He bent his head one way, and the other way.
He moved closer, backed off, and extended his arms,
    searching for new angles between his fingers.

Finally, he delivered his verdict:

      "The composition is accurate,
      the perspective is precise,
      the colours are genuine.
      This is a perfect photograph."

Half an hour later,
    the janitor happened to walk by the door.
She left her pail and her mop in the hallway,
    came in, and walked slowly around the room.
She stood in front of the last photograph on the left,
    looked back for me, and exclaimed:

      "This photo, I'm telling you, it's beautiful!"

Bills

Since their first encounter in 1789,
    Dene and White people
    have argued everywhere and about everything.

This time it was Yenelly and Bertrand, in Pedzéh Kį (Wrigley):

      "You White people, you spoiled our Dene ways."

      "But we did a lot of good."

      "Like what?"

      "Medical care!"

      "You can't even cure the sicknesses you brought to us."

      "Advanced education!"

      "We educated our children for centuries without you."

      "But now they have to learn new ways."

      "So you teach us what we wouldn't need if you had not come."

      "Better transportation!"

      "Now we're like you, going fast to nowhere for nothing."

      "Modern warm clothing!"

      "Yes, but you buy our furs very cheap
        and you get rich selling expensive fur coats."

      "O.K., we made some mistakes, but we did a lot of good."

      "Oh yes, you showed us a few things,
        those things that we don't really need.
      But you never showed us the real stuff.
      You never taught us the important things."

      "Like what?"

      "Like to print dollar bills."

Bingo

I was visiting a small southern town,
    and the Spring sun invited me for a walk.

In front of a church, I noticed a sign:

"You can be part of the World Day of Prayer.
    Today, 7 P.M.,
    at St. John's Church.
    We hope you'll come."

Three blocks further I walked by another church
    with another sign:

    "Bingo tonight, 7 P.M.
    We know you'll come."

Fire

I walk in bitter cold and biting wind,
    my head bent low,
    my neck and my back increasingly stiff.
I am dressed as warmly as usual
    but my lips, my cheeks,
    my hands in my mitts,
    my feet in my boots,
    feel unusually icy.

I decide to stop at Jody's place.
The thought itself warms me up
    and my body relaxes.
My mind focuses less on the cold
    and more on the stove waiting for me.

Jody has just returned from the store.
While sorting out her groceries, she breathes out:
    "A good fire will help me too."

Her wood stove looks like a fireplace
    when a screen replaces the iron door.
It doesn't take me long:
    a small match, a few sparks,
    crackling wood and dancing flames.

    Is it possible I am so cold?
I scrub the frost out of my cheeks.
I knead my hands close to the flames.
I fold and unfold my fingers
    until they colour again
    and burn inside and out.
My eyes start to cry
    as if ice is melting out of me.

I take off my parka, drop it onto the floor.
I rub my hands over my arms and my chest
    and down over my thighs.

I close my eyes, I bend over the stove.
The heat caresses and enters me.

The flames dance and jump,
    curl and shoot straight up.
I am too far, I move closer,
    like a starving man tempted by the juiciest food.
I am too close, I have to back off,
    the heat is intense and could scorch me.
        Fire can be a cruel friend.
        Fire killed Kenny my friend.
        When does one gamble too much?

    I experienced cold so many times before,
        driving my dogteam or snowshoeing all day long.
    I could handle my toboggan with bare hands at minus 20.
    I could sleep outside on a mattress of spruce bows.
    I was young then. I couldn't anymore.

I stand up, I crouch, I rise,
I bend my knees, up and down, up and down.
I feel every joint loosening up
    as if frozen grease is thawing.

        How can heat permeate my body?
        Why does a spruce log burn, and not steel and stones?

I turn my back to the fire.
I can roll my shoulders again
    and twist my frigid neck.
I sit on a stool,
I remove my boots,
I stretch my legs,
I curl my toes up and down.
My blood is flowing freely again.
        'From head to toes' means something after all.

        Stay near the fire?
            all day?
                all night?
                    for ever?

        Oh, Brother Fire!

Slave River, -40°C, downstream from Tthebatthié (Fort Fitzgerald), where the Cassette rapids never freeze, 1985.

Believing

Rose Mary and I were in a talkative mood,
    and we had covered many topics already
    when she declared:

    "I don't believe in God!"

I inquired:

    "What do you believe in?"

She stretched and waved her arms:

    "I believe in the mystery of the stars,
        and in the depth of the oceans.
    I believe in respecting nature,
        in using its resources wisely,
        and in caring for everything I touch."

She smiled:

    "I believe in silence, music, rhythm, and colours,
        the small pebble, the rugged mountain,
        the graceful butterfly, the majestic tree,
        and the life I gave to my two children."

Her eyes sparkled:

    "I believe in the dignity of each person,
        in their intelligence and creative spirit.
    I believe in respect for anyone's choices,
        solidarity and freedom for all people."

She was nearly singing:

> "I believe that each person
>> must fight every alienation,
>> strive towards fullness of life,
>> the destruction of all injustices,
>> and the creation of a more humane world."

She stood up and was ready to dance:

> "I believe in love, the lively children,
>> the committed couples, and the wise elders.
> I believe in the soft skin of my baby,
>> and in the wrinkles of my grandparents.
> I see myself in all, and all in me."

She whispered:

> "But I don't believe in God."

The next day I happened to read
Saint Paul's letter to the Romans (10:20):

> "God said:
>> 'I was found by those who were not looking for me.
>> I appeared to those who were not asking for me.' "

Fish and Sheep

Merle, Magdi, and Marty commented
about Father Wayme's sermon
on the dignity of the priesthood:

> "He used a few big words,
> but he surely knew how to tell the story
> about the shepherd and the sheep."

> "I liked it too but he forgot to mention
> that sheep can be sheep without a shepherd.
> But what's a shepherd without sheep?"

> "My dad, a fine fisherman, used to say:
>   'Fish can be fish without any fisherman around,
>   but what's a fisherman if there is no fish?' "

> "Then, the sheep and shepherd story... Could it mean
> that we can be a parish even without a parish priest,
> but what's a parish priest without a parish?"

Engineer

I boarded the plane, and I discovered a book,
    forgotten in the seat pocket.
It was a collection of short stories;
    one was titled 'Engineer,' and it read:

The president of my company burst into my office.

"Mike! he shouted, we won the $ 300,000,000 contract,
    and we owe that to your skill!
Now, we'll save $ 3,000,000
    if we float the cut stones from the Bretel quarry
    75 kilometres down the river to the building site.
Find a way, Mike."

"That's easy, a few barges and a tugboat."

"No, no! no boat, no raft, no barge!
I want you to float these stones by themselves."

"Yes mister President, if you say so, I will do it."

Deep inside, I knew it couldn't be done.
In all my years as an engineer
    I had never heard of floating stones.
I had read books and books on hydraulics,
    but nobody had thought of that either.

A week later the president called me:

"How are you doing Mike?"

"Not much progress!"

"Hurry up Mike, get at it."

I went at it, and I experimented
    in my bathtub and my swimming pool.

"Mike, we've got to move on that project!"

But I wasn't moving closer to a solution.

"Hi great engineer Mike! any solution yet?"

By then I was wondering
    if I was even a small engineer at all.

"Mike, haven't you got a clue yet?"

I searched, evenings and weekends,
    and I started to wonder why I was searching.

"Mike, I want a report in a week!"

All I could drop on the president's desk
    was a list of the difficulties.
I also dropped my head down.

"Mike, can't you work faster?"

I couldn't work any more, either fast or slow.

"Mike, what about your problem?"

Yes, I myself had become the problem.

"Mike, can't you keep stones from sinking?"

My mind itself was starting to sink.

"Mike, what's wrong with you?"

By then, everything was wrong with me!...

What happened to Mike? How did the story end?
I don't know.
The next two pages of the book had been ripped off.

Back!

In December 1976, I visited Rádełı Kǫ́ę́ (Fort Good Hope),
    where I lived from 1953 to 1960, and also in 1968-1969.
It's always a joy to meet the K'áhshotıne again.
Their name means Big Rabbits' People, or Hareskins.
Hares, always abundant in their territory, provided food,
    and their hides, cut into strips
    were woven into warm clothing and blankets.

Rádełı Kǫ́ę́, a few kilometres from the Arctic Circle,
    is known as the coldest place in Denendeh.
During my one week visit,
    the thermometer stuck at minus 40 degrees,
    and I drank a lot of hot tea in every house.

At the Takalay's home, Jane explained:

> "We were trapping at Canoe Lake since October.
> My husband and two boys came back by skidoo.
> Our two small children and myself,
>   we flew back in a small Cessna, yesterday."

Their oldest boy, fifteen years old,
    had not been mentioned, and I inquired:

> "What about Eddy?"

> "Him? he's coming back with our dogteam.
> He left three days ago, he'll be here soon."

I had travelled the Canoe Lake trail by dog team,
    and I remembered it was one hundred and ten miles.
While the conversation was going on,
    I thought of fifteen year old Eddy,
    travelling by himself for three days,
    setting up his tent every evening at -40,
    having to feed himself and the dogs,
    aware that nobody was closer than fifty miles,
    and that any mistake would be his last one.

As we talked, laughed, and drank tea,
    dogbells rang outside near the house.
Little Ben looked through the frosted window:

    "Eddy is back."

Eddy tied the dogs to their posts and walked in.
The fur around his hood sparkled with frost.
He took his parka off, dropped it onto the floor,
    rubbed his mukluks one over the other,
    walked to face the big woodstove,
    bent over slightly, rubbed his cheeks,
    stretched up, flexed his arms back and forth,
    turned around, bent and stretched his legs,
    turned once more, rolled and relaxed all his muscles,
    inviting the heat to invade his body.

Life was going on in the house:
    baby slept on the couch,
    two children played on the floor,
    a boy prepared a pelt stretcher,
    and mother watched a pot on the stove
    while conversing with me.

After a while she turned to Eddy:

    "You came back?"

    "Yes, I came back."

Such simple words after such a trip!
But what intense pride flowing between mother and son thinking:

    "Of course my son came back, he is a man."

    "Of course I came back, I am a man."

Home

Someone yelled "Fire,"
    and a dozen voices screamed "Fire."

Everybody rushed towards the trailer
    caught in a whirlwind of flames.

All members of the Kearns family had escaped,
    and, even with all their goods blazing away,
    they were thankful that no one was injured.

Friends could only watch silently,
    or offer sympathy to the victims.

The next day I visited the burned out family.
What could I say after such a tragedy?
I tried with the ten-year old daughter:

    "Joan, you must feel terrible without a home."

The young girl knew better:

    "Oh, we still have our home,
    but we have no house to put it in."

Dene Church

"Organizing a local Dene Church?
No problem!

We'll bring
theology professors from P.E.I.,
religious brothers from Nova Scotia,
priests from New Brunswick,
deacons from Newfoundland,
religious sisters from Quebec
liturgy teachers from Alberta,
catechists from Saskatchewan,
gospel singers from Ontario,
sacrament ministers from B.C.
catholic youth from Manitoba."

"But what will all those people do?"

They will explain to the Dene:

"You cannot depend on outside help,
    you have to rely only on yourselves,
    you have to build your own church in your own way."

Rádelą Kǫ́ę́ (Fort Good Hope), 1955, photo: Roger Mahé, o.m.i.

Dene Christmas

I arrived in Denendeh in June 1953
    and my bishop sent me to Rádełį Kǫ́ę́ (Fort Good Hope),
    home to about 275 Denes and 25 Whites.
The village was built in a V shape
    between Jackfish Creek on the east
    and Dehcho (Mackenzie River) on the west.

The houses of the White colony,
    R.C. Mission, R.C.M.P., H.B.C., and D.O.T.,
    lined up on top of the Dehcho bank,
    and overlooked the river for miles.
Most of the Dene houses were squeezed together
    along Jackfish Creek, at the back.

In early November, I was visiting John,
    a Dene in his early twenties:

        "John, I saw some of your drawings, and I like them.
        You are quite an artist. Could you draw something for me?"

        "Anything you like!"

        "That's what I was thinking of:
        The Christmas story has been drawn in many ways.
        Could you draw Christmas night as if it had happened here?"

        "Oh yes! No problem. What's in your mind?"

        "No donkeys here, so let's pretend
            that Joseph and Mary travelled with four dogs
            and a toboggan.
        They came by Old Baldy and they arrived here
            (Old Baldy is a high hill north of the village).

        They asked here and there where they could stay
            but there was no room for them.
        They crossed Jackfish creek,
            pitched their tent on the other side,
            and that's where Jesus was born."

John was drawing on the table with his fingers,
     and thinking aloud:

> "The houses here, the creek, Dehcho there,
> their tent up across... Sure I'll do that."

A week later, I met John:

> "Have you been thinking of your Christmas drawing?"

> "Oh yes, a lot."

A week later:

> "John, any news about your drawing?"

> "Yes, I'll do it."

A week, and another week later:

> "John, Christmas is getting near.
> Will you have time to make your drawing?"

His voice dragged:

> "Yes... I guess I will... I think so."

> "John, you don't feel like doing it, do you?"

> "No, not really."

> "Can you tell me why?"

> "I think so... I mean...
> that drawing doesn't make any sense to me."

> "Oh?"

> "You see,
>   if Mary and Joseph had come to our village,
>   they could have walked into any Dene house,
>   and the people would have said:
>   'Come on in, you're welcome.' "

Fort Freedom

Dan and I were best friends.
We had been raised in the same village,
    we always played, worked, and dreamed together.

Travelling was still laborious in the late sixties
    and we had never been far from our village.
In October 1969, we decided to go and visit Fort Freedom.
It was a long way, but we were young and strong.

We walked and walked until we reached a fork:
    One trail to the right, one trail to the left,
    and the third one more or less straight ahead.
Which one led to Fort Freedom?

We chose the trail to the right.
After we walked three days
    we faced a high vertical cliff.
On both sides also the rock was so steep
    that nobody could ever climb it.
There was only one thing to do.
We turned back, we walked and walked,
    finally we arrived at the fork.

After a long rest, Dan reflected:

      "That trail was too rough and narrow!"

I agreed and I suggested:

      "Let's fix it really good."

With our axes we widened the trail
    all the way to the high cliff.
And I'm telling you,
    walking back to the fork was so easy!

We knew we could still do better,
　　and we walked back to our village.
The government gave us pickaxes, shovels, wheelbarrows,
　　and money to hire four of our friends plus a cook.
We worked for months,
　　but we built a first-class gravel road.
The government gave a pick-up truck to Dan and one to me
　　and we kept driving between the fork and the cliff.
At the most scenic spot on our road,
　　the government built us two beautiful homes
　　and a power plant because we needed T.V. and video games.

Like everybody else we wanted to better our lot,
　　so we decided to pave the road.
It was a big, big project.
I don't remember who prepared the budget,
　　and where the equipment and the money came from,
　　probably from the government.
At last, Dan and I could drive racing cars
　　between the fork and the cliff.

People started to travel more frequently.
Upon reaching the fork and the three directions,
　　they saw that our own road was the easiest one,
　　and they inquired:

　　"Is that the road to Fort Freedom?"

Such endless questioning forced us
　　to put up a sign 'Dead End' on our road.
Finally, Dan and I could travel in peace
　　between the fork and the cliff.

Often, Dan and I, we remember the hardship
　　on that first trip to the cliff,
　　and we glory in the progress we created.

Maybe some day, Dan and I, we will have time
　　to go and visit Fort...Fort...
　　Fort...what's its name?

Here I Sit

In Rádełį Kǫ́ę́, Fort Good Hope,
  every afternoon of Summer 1954,
  Old Kochale sat on top of the high bank
  and watched Dehcho River for hours.
He was old because I was young.
He was probably the age I am now.

What was going on in his mind?
Was he reliving his past
  or dreaming his few years still ahead?
One day I was bold enough,
  or inconsiderate enough:

  "Grandpa, what do you think about?
  Do you pray or what?"

The old Dene lifted his eyes off the great river,
  or off whatever world he was contemplating.
He turned his head slightly towards me
  and whispered in his language:

  "Hejon Wida," that is "Here I Sit,"

As I walked away, I heard unspoken words:

  "I have lived in many places through many years.
  I have now blended all my good days and my bad ones.
  I have united my good friends and the others.
  I have bundled together gifts in and gifts out,
    the family I received from and the family I gave to.
  I entwine sunrise and sunset with my own light.
  I embrace morning breeze, noon storms, evening stillness.
  I have become the person I was called to be.
  I have travelled all my rivers and crossed all my lakes.
  Once more I will land at the right place at the right time."

Then I knew:
"I want to become an old man!"

Birth Control

In the early seventies
    southern doctors and nurses
    visited the land of the Dene
    to preach about birth control.

I remember a two-day workshop in Sǫmbak'è (Yellowknife),
    held, of all places, in the Catholic Church.
Dene and Inuit women
    looked at numerous charts and diagrams
    of what they knew already in a different way.

Southern people were also anxious to learn:

      "What were your traditional methods of birth control?"

      "Don't know."

      "What did your mother or grandmother tell you about it?"

      "Don't know."

      "All you women must have talked about it!"

      "Don't know."

Finally one Inuk woman volunteered:

      "Oh yes, we practiced birth control."

Doctors and nurses pulled out pens and notebooks:

      "What method did you use?"

      "It was foolproof and 100% safe."

      "What was it?"

      "I'm telling you, it worked all the time."

      "Then, tell us what you did."

      "We sent the men hunting."

Catechism

"Tina, I had a five-dollar bill in my drawer.
Do you know what happened to it?"

"Yes mom,
At catechism, I learned that Jesus said:
    'Give to whomever asks from you.'
Well, a beggar came to the door this morning,
    and I gave him the five dollars."

In the afternoon, Tina's mother walked to the school:

"Sister, you teach catechism to my Tina?"

"Yes madam."

"Here's what happened to her.
Do you really teach that to the kids?"

Sister too was surprised:

"Listen, Mrs. Brown,
I teach the kids what Jesus said,
I never told them to do it."

Boxing

My friend Angus has always one more story to tell me,
    and so, one rainy Friday evening, he started:

I woke up and I rushed to the window:

    "Shucks! It's blowing."

My grandfather sat quietly at the table:

    "Breakfast is waiting for you, and I'm ready."

'   "We are going? Wow!"

My grandfather, born in 1882, was Johnny Angus Beaulieu,
    but the baptism book shows that he was also named Eugene.
I guess he needed a few middle names
    because there were so many Johnny Beaulieus.
Me too, I was born in Denínu Kų́ę́ (Fort Resolution),
    and in 1948, I was fourteen.

On Wednesday, Big Jim had told my grandfather:

    "There's a boxing match in Kátł'o Dehe (Hay River),
        on Monday."

and my grandfather had remembered
    that he had some business to do over there.

I knew about boxing from our battery radio,
    but I had never seen a boxing match,
        not even on TV, because there was no TV yet.
Now I was going to see live boxing. Wow!

Grandpa said one boxer was Douglas somebody.
The other one was Fred Lambert,
    a Cree Indian from Peace River country
    who was known to be very strong.
He had two daughters, Martha and Ruby,
    and four boys, good boxers also:
        'Cowboy,' 'Boxer,' 'Punch,' and one more.

My grandfather's brother, Paul,
    had a twenty-two foot boat, with a small cabin.
Joe Charlo also had a boat like that,
    and Alexis Jean Marie, and Johnny Jean Marie.
Our two-cylinder engine was kind of weak:
    it couldn't take us up Buffalo River,
    but, if the wind was right, it was OK on the lake.

That engine had no choke.
We poured a thimble full of gasoline
    into two holes on the top.
We rocked the flywheel back and forth,
    and the gas reached the cylinders with a whizzy sound.
We closed the two holes,
    and a swing of the flywheel started the engine.
Boy, that was a heavy flywheel!

Usually it took one and a half days to Kátł'o Dehe,
    but we decided to leave on Friday.
We couldn't afford to miss that match,
    and you never knew what could happen
    with that engine or with the weather.

The Hay River new town was not built yet,
    and everybody lived on Vale island.
We waited Sunday and Monday for the boxing match,
    but on Monday evening, it was pouring rain.
Because the ring was outside, the match was cancelled,
    and the next day, and the next day.
We couldn't go home without watching the match,
    so, grandpa and I, we waited.

Finally they decided the match would take place
    under a big yellow canvas, at 7 P.M.
My grandfather and I we were at the ring
    at least one hour earlier.
We were used to waiting.
It cost twenty five cents for children,
    and seventy five cents for adults.

Two chairs waited on the ring corners
    because it was to be a real match.
I don't remember the referee's name,
    but Harry Clark rang the bell.

Fred Lambert was a big man, way over two hundred pounds.
I was still a child, so he looked much bigger yet.
Douglas was at least twenty pounds lighter than Fred.
He got onto the ring, jumped up and down,
    threw himself against the ropes,
    and bragged of how he would destroy Fred.
My grandfather started to roll a cigarette
    while keeping his eyes on the ring.

7 o'clock! The bell rang,
    and the two boxers walked towards each other.
Fred whirled on his feet,
    and, with a back swing, he struck his first blow.
Douglas collapsed and lay flat on the mat.
Everybody froze in silence.
My grandfather stopped rolling his cigarette.

    "One, two, three, four, five, six, seven, eight, nine, ten."

The referee announced:

    "That's it folks."

We walked away.
Half to myself and half to grandfather I whispered:

    "Two days sailing, five days waiting,
    two more days to get back...all for nothing."

Grandpa's eyes smiled at me:

    "We had a great time together, boy,
    We had a great time, the two of us, didn't we?"

Jacket

Ben leisurely followed the Yellowknife sidewalks,
   enjoying the gentle sun of September 1988.
He quietly entered the 'Native Arts' store
   and stared at the fancy mitts and slippers:

    "My gosh! So much pretty stuff!"

He gently caressed a moose hide jacket
   and fingered its colourful beads.
Turning around, he shyly faced the store keeper,
   but her eyes were friendly
   and, in a mixture of Chipewyan and English, he explained:

    "You know, I was born in the bush, five miles from here.
    My mom used to make jackets like this one
       for the miners who came here in the forties.
    She was a hard-working woman, my mom!
    I watched her scrape, tan, and stretch dozens of hides,
       and sew millions of beads by candlelight.

    I always dreamt of wearing a moose hide jacket,
       but mom had to sell them all to buy food for us children.
    Then I grew up, I got crippled, sick most of the time,
       and I was two years in Camsell Hospital for T.B.
    That's when my mom died.
    When I came back, my people were good to me,
       they always gave me enough food and a warm place to sleep.
    But I could never afford a moose hide jacket.

    You must sell a lot of things in here.
    Maybe you could help me out.
    I mean, keep that jacket for me till Christmas.
    I think I'll have enough money then
       to pay half of the price,
       and a little bit every month after."

The young clerk was moved by Ben's story,
    but she was only a clerk.
Luckily, the manager walked in.
She was more imposing and Ben felt more shy.
Having listened to his dream she concluded:

    "I will have to talk to the board.
    Due to the unusual circumstances,
        our regularly increasing cash flow,
        and the eventual possibility
        that you could pay in installments..."

Ben lost track of her explanations,
    and he wondered how a board could help him out.

The manager had suggested he could get a loan.
Ben went to one bank, and to another one.
Nobody could interpret into Chipewyan
    the details about collaterals and promissory notes,
    and Ben felt that even the best translation
    would have helped him very little.

The next day, on the post office steps,
    Ben told his friends about the jacket.
They didn't know if they should laugh or cry.
All together they had about twelve dollars in change.

Ben went to the office of a Native association.
He was directed to a second organization,
    thence to a third one which suggested
    he could try the sixteen Yellowknife churches
    and a number of charitable organizations.

Ben walked back to the store.
The presidents of the Native associations,
    the chief negotiator of something,
    and a man called a director were all excited
    about somebody with all kinds of names:
    Prime, Mulroney, Minister, Brian, Honorable:

"He's the best friend the Natives ever had,
    and he's coming to Behchokǫ̀ (Rae) to sign the agreement.
Giving him a moose hide jacket would foster
    the outcome of the negotiation process,
    the welfare of all the Dene around here,
    and the future of all the Aboriginal nations."

So they wanted the nicest jacket
    for the man with many names.
And they would give it to him for free
    because that guy, he needed it so badly!

Ben realized that they wanted 'his' jacket.
He tiptoed out, walked two blocks,
    found himself in front of a church, and entered.
Somebody was reading from a gospel book written by Luke:

"To the man who has, more will be given;
    and from the man who has nothing,
    even the little he thinks he has will be taken away."

Ben started to feel so good, and he smiled:

"At least, that guy is talking straight,
    I never heard so much truth for a long long time."

Maggy Fisher, Rádelı̨ Kǫ́ę́ (Fort Good Hope), 1969.

Maggy was a Hareskin, renowned for her hunting and trapping skills and her artistic beadwork. Her husband Barney Fisher came from the south in the early 1900's and settled in Fort Good Hope. "He never learned a Dene language, their friends recall, and she spoke her own kind of English, so they must have found a way to communicate somehow". Maggy died in 1979 at the age of ninety-five.

Scraping moose hide before tanning, Madeline Catholique and Helen Tobie, 1990.

At the 1971 Indian Ecumenical Conference in Morley, Alberta.

On Tucho (Great Slave Lake), 1973.

Life

I will learn,
change,
grow into freedom to be my Self.

More pressing,
I need to celebrate
what I have received,
what I have become,
who I am,
Life,
Spirit, Creator,
People,
Blessings, Gifts,
Earth,
Love.

I lived the past,
I'll prepare for the future.
Now is now.

Now is to live
coolness and passion,
tears and laughter,
silence and screams
without goal or reason.

Now is to walk, canoe, and swim, not to enhance my health,
simply because the path and the river exist.

Now is to watch the birds, not to learn of freedom and immensity,
simply because we neighbour each other.

Now is to rest, not to refresh my mind,
simply for the joy of resting.

Seasons offer challenges which lead to growth.
Now is the season
    to celebrate my life, my Spirit,
    the strength and weaknesses of my body,
    as it should be now, and as it is.
Now is the season
    to celebrate
    my heart, lungs, eyes, ears, bones,
    and all the other parts
    which I never took time to appreciate,
    but which have been me so well for so long,
        together receiving life,
            growing life,
                sharing life.

Now is the season
    to believe in uselessness,
        do nothing for no reason,
            play, dance, share a kiss,
                feel the water running through my fingers,
                caress a tree,
                    a stone,
                        a blade of grass,
                        a rough hide,
                          a soft skin,
                sing nature's rhythms:
                swirling snow,
                    tender leaves,
                      scorching sun,
                        juicy berries.

Now is the season
    to feel the Spirit present in my history,
        to feel life's surges and passions,
            to trust in life,
                and to accept the risk to lose it
                    (without that risk, it wouldn't be life).

            to laugh at myself,
                to laugh with others,
                    to laugh with the Great Mystery,
                as to laugh is to love.

Yes, there are still roads to travel,
   solutions to find,
      problems to solve,
         knowledge to discover,
            sufferings to alleviate,

But first, I need to thank life,
   respond to life,
      my friends' life,
         nature's life,
            the Spirit's life,
               my life,
                  simply because it is life.

AIDS

How long had Leonard lain in bed?
Longer than a few days,
    longer than many weeks.
His muscles vanished,
    his skin stretched over his bones,
    his face whiter than the white pillow case,
    his eyes as flickering candles at the bottom of a deep well,
    one could say he was alive.
Yes, he was still breathing.

His short life had been a long battle against AIDS.
He, and his mother Martha, knew he had lost the battle.

She helped him turn his head
    and move slightly in his bed.
She wiped the sweat off his face
    and kissed his forehead, gently
    as she had done twenty three years ago
    when he was a newborn baby.
Once again he was her whole universe.

Three years ago Leonard had whispered to her
    that his test was positive,
    and she had held him tightly in her arms.
He had told Gina his girlfriend,
    and she never saw him again.
His dreams faded away:
    a good job, a happy marriage, a joyful home,
    holidays in the sun, Disneyland with the kids,
    peaceful retirement and golden years.

Friends wondered if they could shake hands with him,
    slap him on the back, or have a drink together.
Rapidly they simply disappeared.
Some infection, uncontrollable, invaded his body.
He couldn't drive his car any more,
    play hockey, jog, or even walk around the block.
He stayed home,
    he stayed in his bedroom,
    he stayed in bed.

It used to be a lively home:
    friends, neighbours, visitors,
    music, parties, and games.
Martha, a great cook, now wondered:

        "When was the last time
        I prepared my favorite dishes?"

Former faithful friends and kind neighbours
    were asking one another:

        "How come he turned so bad?
        Why did he spoil his life?
        Couldn't he be more responsible?
        Why didn't she teach him better,
           give him sound advice and proper help?"

Mother and son had been alone for so long
    that she was startled when the doorbell rang.
Letha the visitor, and Martha the mother
    watched the young man fall asleep.
Was it already the sleep of death?

Letha took the mother's hands in hers:

        "How can you still stand on your feet?
        All that time must have been so terrible for you!"

Martha straightened herself up,
    her face drawn but peaceful, her eyes sparkling:

        "Terrible? oh no! he's my son."

Annunciation

"Good morning, my great angel Gabriel,
    but you look so sad!"

"Dear God, there's a reason for it.
You remember that you sent me to Mary.
Well, I just came back from Nazareth."

"Yes, and what?"

"Mary said 'no.' "

"She said 'no'! What happened?"

"I appeared to Mary, who was surprised of course,
    but I had prepared my speech well, and I told her:

      'God has decided to send his son to earth.
      He thought his son should have a queen for a mother,
        but He consulted some of the prophets,
        and guess what? They agreed on you!
      They all said: Mary is so kind, so gracious,
        so bright, so beautiful, and on and on...'

Dear God, I don't know if you asked the prophets,
    but I thought that mentioning them
    would influence Mary the right way.
So I kept on:

      'Mary, you can say yes or no,
        but it will be so good if you say yes.
      You'll have a better life than you have now.
      You'll make quite a name for yourself,
        and all the women will envy you.
      The fate of the world depends on you,
        but feel free to choose what you like.
      And don't be afraid of any problem:
        if you need help, you can call on me.'

Dear God, I explained everything so well;
   but Mary calmly replied:

      'Please, Gabriel, I don't like playing games.' "

God smiled at the angel's report:

   "Gabriel, why did you talk to Mary in such a way?"

   "Dear God, I had never talked to a woman before,
      so, last week, I went to earth looking for advice.
   I met some politicians and religious leaders,
      and I asked them how they manage
      to make people do what they want them to do."

   "Yes, I know how those people operate.
   Gabriel, Mary is a woman of faith,
      and there is no need to bribe or manipulate her.
   Gabriel, I'm sure she has forgiven you.
   Wait a month or so, go and talk to her again,
      with respect."

Gabriel followed God's advice, and Mary answered:

   "May it happen to me as you have offered."

Goats

Jesus addressed a multitude:

> "The Son of Man will sit on his throne...He will divide
> all the earth's people into two groups, just as the shepherd
> separates the sheep from the goats. He will put the sheep at
> his right, and the goats at his left. Then he will say to
> those at his right: 'Come you who are blessed by my Father...'
> He will say to those on his left: 'Away from me, you who are
> under God's curse.'..." (Matthew, ch. 25)

From the back of the crowd, a man raised his voice:

> "Jesus, you are a carpenter,
> and your friends are fishermen.
> I've been raising sheep and goats all my life,
> and I'm asking you:
>
>> What's right about sheep?
>> What's wrong about goats?
>
> The Book of Truth says that the Creator made everything good,
> and I'm telling you:
> He created the goats especially good:
>
> Goats are such pure animals
> that they can carry the people's sins away to the desert.
>
> Goats were the first ruminants to be domesticated. In the time of
> Abraham, goat herding was already more important than
> agriculture. Right now, goats are still the most common
> domesticated animals.
>
> Goats can scramble up sheer cliffs. Goats do well on the poorest
> lands, where sheep and all other animals would starve.
> Goats, with the toughest mouth of all ruminants, and with
> four stomachs, can eat tough grass, nettles, thistles, briers,
> bushes, and brambles.

Goats give us meat and milk, and goat milk is the only milk naturally homogenized. Goat hair is woven into clothes. Goat horns are carved into trumpets. Goats' skins provide leather, tents, drum tops, food, water and wine containers.

Goat kids, unlike most animals, are born with their eyes open and right after birth, they can stand and walk. And, all of you farmers and herders, you know that goats are cleaner animals than cows, sheep, pigs, chickens, and even dogs. Some people may dislike the odor secreted by buck goats, but the other goats don't object to it.

Goats are social animals. When goats are feeding, at least one of the herd stands guard against possible predators. Goats respond to human friendship, even to the point of giving milk only for the people they like.

Now, Jesus, I heard that you cured some people, and you improved the sight of a few others. But when you're not around, that's what we do. When my boy Jonathan burned his arm, goat marrow cured him. Goat milk cured the swollen tonsils of my daughter Naomi. When my mother suffered from insomnia, I cured her by rubbing the gallbladder of a goat doe under her eyes. My father-in-law's failing sight improved when my wife applied soft goat cheese to his eyes.

Jesus, you know a lot,
    and I like most of what you say,
    but listen to a long time herder:

Goats were created to be goats,
    to be what goats are supposed to be,
    and to do what goats are supposed to do.

And I'm telling you and all the people here:
    All the goats will be on the right side...
    and, I guess, all the people too."

Truck lights

Winter time and very cold,
    early afternoon but already dark.
I'm driving from Sǫmbak'è (Yellowknife) to Behchokǫ̀ (Rae)
    in my 15-year old pick-up truck,
    and a Dene elder asked me for a ride.

The land has taught the Dene
    to live in a world of silence.
After ten kilometres, Kolchia reflects:

    "Driving the truck is like having faith in God."

I'm trying to figure out what he means,
    but, after two kilometres I give up:

    "Grandpa, you talked about driving and faith in God.
    I'm not sure what you meant."

Kolchia turned slightly towards me:

    "You started the engine and you put the lights on.
    We could have said:
       'We see only one hundred metres ahead.
       Further on, it's one hundred kilometres of darkness,
         so we cannot go to Behchokǫ̀.'

    But you got the truck into gear,
       we started to move,
       and the lights kept showing ahead of us.
    Must be the way with God too
       who shows us only a bit into the future,
       just enough for our next move.
    If we are afraid and if we stand still,
       we'll never see further ahead.
    But if we go with the little light we have,
       the light keeps showing us the way on and on."

Coca Cola

In Manila, Ramon, Mirasol, Elsa, Celia, and Ben
   were reflecting on the history of the Philippines,
   and discussing the future of their nation:

> "Foreign speculators have exploited our resources and
> shattered our economy."

> "The political and cultural imperialism of First World
> countries has brainwashed us."

> "We will dismantle evil colonialism and neo-colonialism."

> "We will regain total control of our economy from the greed
> of imperialistic America."

> "We will tear apart the web of lies created by foreign
> power elites."

> "We will shape our own domestic and foreign policies."...

During their passionate conversation,
   they had drunk eleven bottles of Coca-Cola.

Coca-colanization?

Texaco

In 1980, I took part in a three-week seminar
    organized in Trinidad and Tobago,
    a country of only 4,900 square kms.

Like many 'Islands in the Sun,'
    Trinidad and Tobago are full of contradictions.
One conspicuous contradiction
    occupied the south west corner of Trinidad:
    the third largest refinery in the world.

I was explained that Middle East oil
    was refined here and shipped to the United States.
It was a matter of tax evasion, cheap labor,
    and lack of pollution control.
Obviously, the refinery
    held as much power as the national government.

I was not allowed to visit the refinery,
    but I peeped through the barbed wire fence:
Luxurious houses and swimming pools,
    manicured gardens, lawns and sprinklers,
    golf courses and fancy limousines.
I felt like being in Texas, which was normal:
    the refinery belongs to Texaco.

One Sunday, in a large church near the refinery,
    I celebrated Mass in front of people
    from the palest blond to the blackest black,
    from every race, nation, and language.

After Mass, in front of the church,
    people questioned me about Canada, about snow,
    about my ministry, about Aboriginal Nations.

One girl, possibly eighteen years old,
    with blue eyes and golden hair, addressed me:

"Next month I'm going to Canada for my holidays."

I inquired: "Are you from Canada?"

She smiled: "No, I'm not from Canada."

"Are you from the United States?"

She shook her head: "No. I'm not."

I got more curious and I asked:

"Are you from Trinidad?"

"Oh no, she said, I'm from Texaco."

Democracy

1967 in Denendeh!
Five caribou were crossing a frozen lake.
Far behind, a black dot was following,
    which rapidly grew into a wolf.
Before the caribou started to run,
    the wolf spoke to them, which was unusual.
Still more unusual were his words:

> "Brothers, you and I have suffered
>   from much violence between your race and mine.
> Our ignorance of democracy caused our troubles.
> I have learned about democracy in the south,
>   and I will teach you:
>
> In a democracy, decisions are taken by voting.
> I will give you your first lesson in democracy.
> If you want to vote 'yes,' you howl on a high note.
> If you want to vote 'no,' you howl on a low note.
> You heard me howling, start practicing."

Two caribou howled quite well.
Two produced odd but acceptable sounds.

> "Obviously, said the wolf,
>   the fifth caribou will never howl properly.
> He will never be able to vote,
>   and he will slow down our progress in democracy.
> Don't you agree that he should be eliminated?
> Thank you. I will implement your decision.
>
> My four dear brothers, you need an education.
> The most important things are figures and numbers.
> Today I'll teach you to count to five."

Two caribou made it past three.
One managed: "one-two, one-two."
One repeated only :"one-one-one."

> "Our brother, concluded the wolf,
>   will never get an education.
> He will become a drop-out,
>   which would be a disgrace to us all...
> Thank you. I will implement your decision.
>
> My dear three brothers,
>   in a democracy everyone needs to compete.
> We will have a race."

The wolf came first.
Two caribou made it to the finish line.
One was so far behind
    that, no doubt, he would always flunk.

> "We must prevent our brother from becoming a failure...
> Thank you. I will implement your decision."

One of the remaining two caribou complained:

> "I have my doubts about education and democracy."

His brother caribou asked advice from the wolf
    which agreed that a single dissident would slow the progress.

> "My last dear brother, said the wolf,
> you who learned so rapidly about democracy,
> I'll lead you to the best feeding ground I know."

Both agreed democratically,
    and they reached a place without any moss at all.
The last caribou, weaker and weaker, pleaded with the wolf:

> "Brother, I won't live much longer.
> If you eat me up, you at least can survive
>   and teach democracy to all the other Caribou in Denende

Forever

During a land claim negotiation meeting,
the Minister of Indian Affairs addressed the Dene:

"Your fatherland covers 1,000,000 square kilometres,
and you possess all rights over those 750,000 kilometres.

As long as the sun shines,
you may occupy those 600,000 kilometres.
As long as the river flows,
you may roam freely over your 400,000-kilometre heritage.
However, your 200,000 kilometres are part of Canada,
and Canadian laws will prevail over your 100,000-kilometre land.

In case non-Dene settle on your 50,000-kilometre domain,
and want to share the resources of your 20,000 kilometres,
my government will protect you anywhere
within the boundary of your 1,000-kilometre region.
Your children too may live for ever on your 500 kilometres,
in guaranteed security on your 100-kilometre territory.

Following our agreement about your 50-kilometre tract,
I will provide you with a Canadian flag
which you may fly anywhere on your 10-kilometre property,
as a sign of our friendship treaty regarding those 5 kilometres.

Even if the national interest requires
that you give up the one square kilometre you own,
I will ensure that you will still have enough land
on which you can stand and fly a kite."

Divisions

On the third evening of the Dene National Assembly,
I was drinking tea in Tchinkon's tent.

After a long period of silence he inquired:

"René, how do you feel?"

"I'm not sure."

Most Dene in the tent joined in:

"I'm not as enthusiastic as before."
"We don't seem to know what we want."
"Regions argue among themselves."
"It's not like in the seventies."
"Villages blame each other."
"Former friends have become strangers."

My host prodded me again:

"Aren't you discouraged?"

"I lived with worse divisions before.
In 1940, the German army invaded two-thirds of France.
Our nation was divided into an 'occupied' zone, and a 'free' zone,
     but our government had real power over neither one.

Some French businessmen were pragmatic
     and welcomed the enemy's goals, ideas, and policies:

'The Nazis have conquered half of Europe.
They are strong, they are here to stay.
We need to lower our ideals, and to compromise.
At least, we can get jobs in factories,
     and we have the opportunity to make good money.'

Some women also seized the opportunities.

Other French people, the idealists, proclaimed:

> 'Our land is invaded, but not our hearts.
> We still are a great nation.
> We still speak our own language.
> We still have our glorious past, and a great future.
> We cannot fight with guns, but we'll fight in other ways.'

Many joined le maquis, the underground.
Thousands suffered and died for their ideals,
    knowing that freedom was worth more than even their own lives.
Some of my neighbours were snatched out of their homes at night,
    taken to concentration camps, starved, beaten to death,
        never heard from again.

The pragmatists laughed at such martyrs:

> 'Why didn't they keep quiet?
> Why didn't they accept the rules of the game?
> They got what they deserved.'

Families were split, man against woman, mother against daughter.
Louis, one of my friends joined the underground at 18.
He lived in hell for two years and he lost one hand
    while his father was making a few million francs
        through 'good deals' with the occupation army.
At the Liberation, in 1944, my friend shot his dad...

When I visited France last year,
    forty years after the war,
    I saw German children in French schools,
    and French girls married to German boys.

If French and Germans are now friends
    after killing each other by the millions for centuries,
    the Dene will work out their quarrels too."

Masks

I glanced, horror-stricken.
Instinctively all my nerves tensed up.

Everything in that face shocked me, disturbed me, repulsed me:
    glaring eyes, crooked nose, uneven ears, sagging cheeks,
    protruding teeth, cavernous mouth, greenish colours.

I could not back off
    but I didn't want to get any closer.

Guess who was wearing
    that repulsive Halloween mask ?

Little Jimmy who, even his parents agree,
    is the kindest, the most beautiful, and the most charming child.

On the next day, November 1st., All Saints' Day,
    we read from the first Letter of the apostle John:

        "What we are, all of us,
            [behind our crazy ways and stupid behaviours]
            has not yet been revealed."

Pretending

"Our Mont Royal Park has been so beautiful this summer."

"Oh yes, with plenty of sunshine and enough rain."

"I could feel my branches stretching longer every day."

"My leaves had never been so large and so pretty."

"Quite a few families picnicked near by,
      and many children ran around for hours."

"I remember the two teenagers who spent a night on the grass.
How I listened to their happiness!"

"Unfortunately, Fall is upon us!
Some of our neighbours wear red and yellow leaves already."

"At least we're lucky to be so colourful.
I heard that birch leaves turn only yellow.
It must be monotonous."

"Tell me, why do we let seasons change us?
Can't we refuse Fall and Winter,
      and keep on with our Summer life?"

"We could pretend that Summer is lasting,
      and retain our green leaves."

"After all, the pine trees don't change in winter."

"I even learned that people sing to their trees:
      'Your boughs so green in Summer time
      brave the snow of Winter time.' "

"Then, it's quite easy.
Let's pretend that we are pine trees,
        and everybody will celebrate us also."

"Our neighbours will wonder all through Winter
        why we are the only two maple trees with green leaves."

"What a marvelous dream!
Yet I'm not sure I want to live it.
I feel that I will miss something so beautiful,
        something I have always enjoyed so much."

"What are you talking about?"

"You see, if we refuse Fall and Winter,
        we won't live any Spring either."

Be not afraid

In my middle class parish we often sing a hymn about God's
    promises:
"BE NOT AFRAID...I GO BEFORE YOU ALWAYS."

Really, how many of us will in the near future cross a barren desert,
    pass through raging waters, and walk amid burning flames...?

"BE NOT AFRAID...
YOU SHALL CROSS THE BARREN DESERT, BUT YOU SHALL NOT DIE OF THIRST."

    or, dear God, are you trying to tell us:

"You shall go to oversupplied parties, but you shall not drink
    yourself to stupidity."
"You shall cross the supermarket, but you shall not be lured by all
    the attractive items."
"You shall read glossy advertisements, but you shall not be seduced."?

"BE NOT AFRAID...
YOU SHALL WANDER FAR IN SAFETY, THOUGH YOU DO NOT KNOW THE WAY."

    or, dear God, are you trying to tell us:

"You shall follow me, though you haven't done a feasibility study, or
    a cost analysis."
"You shall walk towards freedom with the oppressed,
    though you do not know for how many more miles."
"You shall believe in the future, though you have
    no insurance policies, no long term deposits, and no retirement fund."?

"BE NOT AFRAID...
YOU SHALL SPEAK YOUR WORDS TO FOREIGN MEN, AND THEY WILL
UNDERSTAND."

or, dear God, are trying to tell us:

"You shall listen to the oppressed, the street people, the aboriginal
people, and the bag ladies, and you will understand."
"You shall listen to the winds, marvel at a flower, feel the sunshine,
walk in the dew, and it will make sense."
"You shall ignore trends and fashions, and you will understand your
own life."?

"BE NOT AFRAID...
YOU SHALL SEE THE FACE OF GOD, AND LIVE."

or, dear God, are you trying to tell us:

"You shall look at a drunk with respect, and you both will see me."
"You shall laugh with the children and cry with the sorrowful,
and you will all feel like me."
"You shall open your door at 11 P.M., not knowing who has
knocked, and I will be there."?

"BE NOT AFRAID...
IF YOU PASS THROUGH RAGING WATERS, IN THE SEA YOU SHALL NOT DROWN."

or, dear God, are you trying to tell us:

"If you walk in the muddy shoes of my friends, you shall be
cleansed."
"If you join others in their stormy lives, you shall find rest."
"If you raise a raging storm against unjust situations, you shall be
pacified."

"BE NOT AFRAID...
IF YOU WALK AMID THE BURNING FLAMES, YOU SHALL NOT BE HARMED."

    or, dear God, are you trying to tell us:

"If you leave your fireplace to spread the fire I brought to the
    earth...
If you challenge the unconscious, the unaware, and the contented...
If you stand up to the powerful, disturb the specialists, and scorn
    wealth, ... you shall not be harmed."?

"BE NOT AFRAID...
IF YOU STAND BEFORE THE POWER OF HELL, AND DEATH IS AT YOUR SIDE,
KNOW THAT I AM WITH YOU THROUGH IT ALL."

    or, dear God, are you trying to tell us:

"If you are ridiculed by the army, business, and political circles,
    I will laugh it off with you."
"If you are ignored or rejected by the religious authorities, you will
    still love them with my own love."
"If you life ends in total failure, like mine, know that Easter is
    only two nights away."

On your way!

Our dear sons and daughters,
    since you were born,
    we have guided you prudently
    and ensured that you would never get lost.

The highway we built for you
    required our engineering talent,
    our skilled labour, and our powerful equipment.
We had to blast rocks, fill up muskegs,
    level a few hills, and even dig four tunnels.

We taught you safety rules
    and mechanical secrets.
Now, we give you this beautiful car
    which is perfectly suited to your needs.

Use any kind of gasoline you like,
    Gulf, Esso Super, Petro Canada.
Drive fast or slow,
    and stop whenever you feel like it.

Study the map we prepared for you,
    read our signs and follow our highway.

After planning everything for you,
    we want you to be independent,
    and to travel on your own.
Be on your way.

Margaret

God said:

"Welcome here, Margaret.
Let's have a look at the big book.
Margaret... from Yellowknife...
one of the street people... Here we are:
swearing, fistfights, drunkenness...
that kind of stuff...

Let me look further...Margaret?

DIDN'T
speculate on my land,
use political patronage,
manipulate the stock market.
live an extravagant lifestyle.

NOT ACCOUNTABLE FOR
the irresponsible uranium mining,
the Airforce low level flights,
the war games and the CF-18's bases,
the militarization of Denendeh and Nunavut.

NOT LIABLE FOR
the unjust justice structures,
the failure of the school systems,
the degrading correction services,
the crooked Land Claims negotiation process.

NOT RESPONSIBLE FOR
the inflation rate,
the ugly Yellowknife skyline,
the increasingly high cost of housing,
the eccentric Frame Lake South subdivision.

NEVER
misused public funds,
devised shady business deals,
cheated on business partners,
used inside information for her own profit.

DIDN'T CONTRIBUTE TO
the pollution of Yellowknife Bay,
the destruction of the environment,
the debt burden in the Third World,
the annihilation of Aboriginal cultures.

Not a bad record, my dear.
Indeed! A very good record in these days!
Welcome here, Margaret."

Opinions

After my first seven years in Denendeh,
    I told the Dene in Rádełı̨ Kǫ́ę́ (Fort Good Hope)
    that I was going to France for my holidays.
They looked at me strangely
    as they had never learned
    to divide their life into work and leisure.
So I said that I was going to visit my mother,
    and it made sense to them.

On my first afternoon in France, I met Loulou:

      "René, what happened to you?
      You look worn out and exhausted.
      It must have been terrible up there.
      Did you starve sometimes?
      I never thought you could have changed so much."

In the evening, I met Maurice, another friend:

      "René, wow! you look great!
      I was afraid life would be tough for you,
         but ice and snow must be your friends.
      Must be a healthy place up there.
      You don't look a day older than seven years ago!"

Such Potential

"You know, Doreen, it hurts me
　　to see so many Dene wasting their lives."

"I feel as sad as you, Tina,
　　there is so much to do in every community."

"Some of those were so smart when they were young."

"And their friends trusted them."

"Many could have become great leaders for their people."

"As their parents or their grandparents were."

"Now they seem to be in neutral."

"Or drifting in every direction."

"They do so little."

"Or things so useless."

"Something must have happened to them."

"They were probably led astray."

"Yes, and I don't want to blame them."

"But there's so much potential wasted!"

"On the other hand, a few Dene
　　have made it in politics and in business."

"Weren't you talking of those?"

Serenity

It took many celebrations
    to inaugurate the new community hall
    which the Dene built at Dettah in the summer of 1970.
Those were the days when, if you wanted something,
    you built it yourself, and you were proud of it.

At Christmas time, in the new hall,
    eight drummers beat the drums,
    and sang at the top of their voices,
    leading three hundred Dene into passionate dancing.

Two drunks from Yellowknife walked in,
    both seemingly unknown to the Dene.
They tried to dance but could hardly walk.
They screamed and yelled as only drunks can do.

The drums kept beating, the singers singing,
    but slowly the dancing circle vanished,
    and the Dene sat down quietly along the walls,
    while the two men kept acting up in the centre of the hall.

Tsetta, sitting next to me, whispered:

    "We were having a good time."

I volunteered a solution:

    "Why don't you kick them out?"

Tsetta shook his head:

    "Why add to their trouble?
    Don't you think they are pitiful enough as they are?"

The drunks kept acting up and yelling
    while everybody else sat silently, as if unconcerned.

When the two got tired of their own show, they walked out.
In ten seconds, the dance was on again.

Prayers

Some of my friends shared with me
the best prayers they said or heard:

"Mom, the stars are smiling at me."

"Ah, the song of that waterfall!"

"Let's splash each other in the pool!"

"Mom, the water is the same shape as the glass!"

"Daddy, don't cut another tree!"

"How does a big tree learn how to make a small tree?"

"Daddy, look at the other side of the lake.
    All the trees stand exactly at the right place."

"How come bones can grow?"

"It's our first kiss!"

"We swam side by side just for the fun of it."

"I walked one hour with my friend,
    and neither of us said a word!"

"Vern made me rediscover the beauty of that book."

"Gill and I looked at our first baby.
Everything we have had before is nothing."

"That street lady shared her stories with me!"

"Per chance, I met that birdwatcher
   and he helped me discover a 'special' bird."

"I was so surprised at what I wrote."

"Why has Johnny the freedom to get stone drunk?"

"Why do people accept being colonized?"

"My God, I don't deserve it."

"God, you're so far away. Did I move?"

"God, comfort me so I can be a comforter."

"God, save me from my worst enemy: apathy."

"Emily listened to a manipulative preacher
   and she raged: 'You phony.' "

"Dennis walked out of the West Edmonton mall
   and he screamed: 'My God, will you ever forgive us?' "

"Cynthia and I watched two hundred hungry men
   waiting for food at the door of a Vancouver convent,
   and she exclaimed: 'If only there were a God.' "

Bible

"Look at my shelves!
I've got them all:

    La Bible de Jerusalem,
    The Revised Standard Version,
    The Douay Version,
    The First Ecumenical Edition,
    The New English Bible,
    The American Standard Version,
    The King James Version,
    La Sainte Bible de Maredsous,
    The Bible in Pictures,
    The Good News Bible,
    Good News for Modern Man,
    The Living New Testament,
    The Amplified New Testament, etc...

    Look at these old manuscripts,
    plus biblical research in nine languages,
    and complete collections of biblical reviews, etc..."

"The Bible must be the guiding light of your life!"

"I'm so busy collecting volumes,
    searching book stores and auction sales.
How could I have time to read anything?"

Priest

The film "The Honour of All"
    describes the worst years on the Alkali Lake reserve, B.C.,
    when men, women, children, elders,
    chief, councillors, and the priest, were abusing alcohol.

The film also shows chief Andy Chelsea,
    his wife Phyllis, and brother Ed Lynch
    celebrating their first year of sobriety:

        "I'm discouraged! After one year, we are only three."

        "That's great! Three more than a year ago."

Sobriety spread steadily over the Alkali Lake reserve.
By 1975, 40% of the Indians were sober, now 90%.

Andy and Phyllis Chelsea came to Yellowknife
    with a rough cut of "The Honor of All."
They showed the film to a few people,
    and asked for comments and suggestions.

At the end of the discussion, I asked Andy:

        "What happened to the Oblate priest we saw in the film?"

        "He went to a treatment centre and recovered.
        He obtained a dispensation and married.
        He became a chemical dependency counsellor,
            as well as a family counsellor,
            and has worked in Maple Ridge, B.C.
        He was responsible for planning and erecting
            a new treatment facility for men and women.
        I think he's starting to become a priest."

Verna Crapeau and her Son in Dettah.

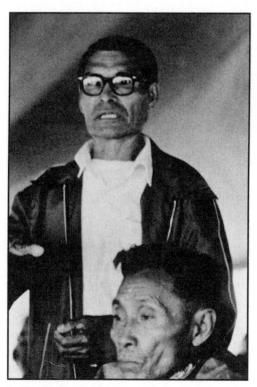

Joe Charlo, Dettah chief in the 1970s.

Ice and snow on Tucho (Great Slave Lake) near Denínu Kų́ę́ (Fort Resolution), 1969.

Lourdes

It is July 17, 1989.
I prayed in Lourdes for the first time in 1939.
Fifty years have brought many changes
    but not much difference.

Some stores pretend to praise Mary:

       'Magasin des Apparitions,'
       'Mary's Two Golden Roses,'
       'Notre Dame du Perpetuel Secours.'

Other stores pray the litany of the Saints:

       'Magasin St. Augustin,' 'Magasin Ste. Anne,'
       'Ste. Rita,' 'St. Paul,' 'Ste Marguerite Marie,'
       'St. Benoit,' 'St. Pascal,' 'St. Francois Xavier,'
       'le Bon St. Christophe,' 'le Père de Foucault.'
       Even more pretentious: 'By God's Grace.'

Religious pictures and 60-cent candles
    mingle with plastic tanks and G.I. Joe's outfits.
A store offers cognac, whisky, liquors,
    and empty plastic bottles to carry Lourdes' water home.

The hotel nearest to the grotto
    where Mary proclaimed: 'Penance'
    is a * * * *, with $ 160 rooms.

The sun is scorching,
    and the waiters repeatedly shout:

       "Two draughts, two!"

Children run from one fountain to the next.
Parents haven't changed either:

       "Come on, hurry up, let's go."

Every day welcomes
    10,000, 15,000, or 20,000 pilgrims:
    Scottish boy scouts following their bagpipes,
    Irish from the Connor diocese,
    French from Lille, Cambrai, and Angoulême.

I wonder at a richly decorated pennant: 'B.B.'
    ...an organization of Belgian farmers.

Msgr. Gaillot, bishop of Evreux,
    often labelled 'the French rebel,'
    prays the rosary with his flock.

Italians from UNITALSI, Pouilles, Catania,
    Cagliari, and Sezione Siciliana Orientale,
    pray with their hands.

Pilgrims kneel in front of the grotto;
    one of the few places in the world
    where anybody can weep without shame.

Two men of the Dutch 'restive church,'
    carry a 40-kilo candle on their shoulders.
Would that be the most efficient weapon
    to start a true revolution?

An old man struggles at every step,
    pushing the wheelchair of his paralyzed wife.

Four children frolic around their parents.
On the father's arms lies the fifth one
    looking as a dishevelled ragdoll.

A young woman, immobilized on a stretcher,
  wears an immaculate white cap
    with brilliant red and blue letters:
    'FERRARI TEAM,' the prestigious racing cars.
Is she on her way to winning
    one of life's real races?

Once in a while a sick person is cured,
    and 9,999 others return home,
    still suffering, but stronger and more alive.

My mother prayed in Lourdes a few times,
    in a wheelchair pushed by a friend.
She had faith in Mary, and faith in herself.

During the evening candlelight procession,
    the rosary is prayed in French, English,
    Dutch, German, Ukrainian, Chinese, Italian,
    and in one African language whose name I forgot.
Mary understands it all.

Three days ago, July 14, in Paris,
    the deadly tanks DM12 and ST27
    were parading, five abreast, on the Champs Elysées.

On the Lourdes esplanade,
    400 wheelchairs and stretchers
    also progress five abreast.
Every year, hundreds of men and women
    dedicate two or three weeks of their holidays
    to wheel and care for the sick.
Priority to the invalid and the most vulnerable!
Priority to all victims of 'good' or 'bad' sicknesses!

What makes our world more human,
    the July 14 wealth and might
    or the Lourdes' poor and infirm?

Watching Jean Delannoy's film 'Bernadette'
    I learned of this 1854 dialogue
    between the local bishop and her:

        "Why do you think Mary has chosen you?
        You are poor and you have no education."

        "If there had been a girl poorer than me,
        Mary would probably have chosen her."

Whether you buy a nine-franc candle,
   or a 24-kilogram, $140 candle, the sign reads:

   "Your candle is a sign of your prayer,
   an offering for the sanctuaries,
   a participation in the Church throughout the world."

And our world is very large.
The Missionary Pavilion reminds us
   that 60% of the world population live in Asia,
   and by the year 2000,
   75% of the Christians will live in Latin America.

Around the altar of the underground basilica
   four torches throw up flames half a meter high,
   symbols of the true light and life.
Waiting for mass, some people argue wildly
   to reserve choice places for their friends.
Others give up their seat with a smile.
Ten bishops and one hundred and fifty priests
concelebrate, wearing waves of white hair.
Flags, pennants, and banners
   sprout up like Spring flowers
   and lead us around the world:
   'Jeunes Young Jugend,'
   'China,' 'Poland,' 'Ukraine,' 'Switzerland,'
   'Luxembourg,' 'Philippines,' 'Jerusalem.'

The choir is Swiss, but the whole world answers:

   "Alleluia"

Can-Afford?

The northern mountains of the Philippines
    are home to one million Aboriginal people, the Igorots.
    I roamed over their territory for one month
    and they enchanted me with their hospitality.

A family of the Aplay tribe
    spoiled me with their kindness and friendship.
Mike is a priest of the Episcopalian Church,
    Sunny is a teacher at the local high school.
Both are outstanding professionals
    but with meager salaries, even by Filipino standards.
They raise pigs, ducks, and chickens
    in order to have meat on the table.
However, they and their four children,
    Sigrid, Wagah, Damey, Bogan,
    are satisfied with their simple life style.

A few 40-watt light bulbs led me to ask:

    "When did you get electricity?"

    "In 1985."

As the climate is constantly hot, I inquired:

    "Are you going to get a refrigerator?"

Both parents smiled in a way which meant
a fridge had been discussed previously.
One answered me:

    "You came with us to many homes here in Kin-Iway,
    and in the neighbouring villages."

    "Yes, and no one could have better introduced me
    to so many Igorots. All are your friends."

"In all the homes we visited,
    how many fridges did you see?"

"I didn't pay much attention,
    but not many."

"As most people, we cannot afford a fridge.
But even if we had the money,
    would it be proper for our family
    to be one of the few 'can-affords'?"

Full circle

You know, René, White people told us Dene:

> "You shouldn't live in tents
>   as savages do. Live in houses."

But whenever they can, they go camping.

White people told us:

> "Do not live in log buildings
>   as savages do. Live in plywood houses."

But wealthy Whites build log mansions.

White people told us:

> "You shouldn't cook on campfires
>   as savages do. Use electric stoves."

But whenever possible, they barbecue outside.

White people told us:

> "Don't paddle your canoes and boats
>   as savages do. Buy outboard motors."

But they paddle their canoes and kayaks for fun.

White people told us:

> "Do not dress in animal hide and fur
>   as savages do. Wear nylon and permapress."

But they glory in their fur coats and stoles.

White people told us:

> "Do not be like savages.
> Follow our dressing code, and be stylish."

But they're naked at the beach and at their cottages.

Still, White people tell us:

> "We are logical, you are dreamers.
> We think with our heads, you get lost in your feelings.
> We follow straight lines, and you zigzag all over."

René, I can't figure it out.

Shampoo

"Excuse me, young lady, do you work here?"

"Yes madam. Can I help you?"

"I need some advice about shampoos."

"Yes madam, here is the 'Silk Protein Shampoo.' "

"Sorry, protein is about food, not hair."

"The 'Alberto European Shampoo' is popular."

"You mean, you have nothing Canadian?"

"Oh yes, the 'Wheat Germ, Oil, and Honey Shampoo.' "

"It sounds more like salad dressing to me."

"Here's the 'Dry Scalp Head and Shoulders.' "

"Are you laughing at me? Do I have a dry scalp?"

"You may like the 'Aussie Shampoo with Papaya.' "

"It's a waste to use papayas in shampoos."

"This is the new 'Sea Mist Shampoo
    with Kelp Protein.' "

"With kelp? It must stink awful."

"Have you ever tried the 'Egg Shampoo'?"

"Are you sure it's made from fresh eggs?"

"That's a favorite: the 'VO5 Extra Body Shampoo.' "

"Do you mean my hair doesn't have enough body?"

"We have the 'Monoi Hawaiian Shampoo,'
    monoi is the name for coconut oil."

"I've never liked coconut."

" 'Timotei Shampoo with Honey and Herbs Extracts' here,
'Balsam Shampoo with Vitamin E' there,
'Aloe Vera Shampoo' on the top shelf,
'Ivory Shampoo' just below,
    and...."

"You mean that's all you have?
I guess I'll try somewhere else.
Thanks just the same."

Housing

All day long, it had snowed in Edmonton.
Charlie slowed his car
    and eased carefully to the sidewalk.
A woman was dragging her feet
    and her shoes half-filled with snow.

    "You going far?" Charlie asked

    "Not too much."

She stepped towards the car,
    fumbled with the door handle,
    and let herself drop onto the front seat.

    "What's your address?"

    "Just keep driving."   A bit later:

    "Turn right...Keep going...
    Turn left...Go a bit more...Stop."

Charlie helped her out of the car:

    "Is that your house?"

    "Um."

They entered a narrow hallway,
    with five doors on each side.

    "No! she said, downstairs."

The shaky steps were tricky,
    and the slimy floor slippery.
The hallway was like the upstairs one,
    but the stink more shocking.
Two doors were ajar,
    probably because they had no lock.

The third door on the right was half open.
The woman stopped, and Charlie asked:

    "Is that where you live?"

Before she could reply,
    a rough voice,
    in a despairing tone,
    answered from behind the door:

    "No, that's where we die."

Anything goes?

"Hi Colin, it's over thirty years since we were in school.
I hated school, I had to cheat my way to grade 12."

"It's OK, everybody needs grade 12!"

"Then I joined the army: it was so much fun learning
    to blast buildings, to blow up cars, to shoot down planes."

"Truly exciting for a young man!"

"I volunteered for the war in Narola.
From planes and helicopters
    we strafed, bombed, and blew up whole villages.
You should have seen those people running like crazy,
    but we shot them like sitting ducks."

"It's one way to get rid of those bastards."

"The war over, I worked with an arms dealer.
I travelled all over: Bamela, Korduran, Zanibo...
Gosh! we made fantastic deals with those countries."

"Certainly a good boost for our economy!"

"I went into real estate.
I tore down old buildings where only poor folks lived,
    and I built fancy condominiums and fabulous mansions."

"Good! We need progress!"

"Then I was in the oil business.
What amazing deals I made with Third World countries!
They trusted any promise, and they signed anything."

"If they are so stupid, that's their problem."

"My next step was politics.
I planned the overthrow of the government in Chamor
    to protect our banks and our plantations there.
Everything was like a kids' game."

"You had a rich and successful life,
    but, how was your family life through all that?"

"My wife and I, we had our ups and downs
    but we managed quite well.
Though, I remember one evening in Calabar,
    I was so tired, so frustrated, so lonesome.
I met a girl, so attractive, I spent the night with her.
The only time in my life I did such a thing."

"You did that! How disgusting! How immoral of you!"

Jean Tinqui of Behchokǫ̀ (Rae), 1975.

Birchbark Church

In the old days, the Aboriginal people of Canada
    paddled their birchbark canoes to Eternity.
They were strong paddlers, and they could find their way
    around thousands of reefs, islands, and sandbars.
Oh yes, it was kind of slow, and some got lost at times.

The Heavenward Company arrived in Denendeh
    with power boats and large barges
    run by male and female specialists.
The captains were always on schedule
    and they set an infallible course for everyone.
The Dene, ignorant about engines and fuel supplies,
    sat quietly in the boats and barges.

A few Dene learned about motors and maintenance,
    but by then, the Heavenward Co. had better specialists,
    more powerful engines, more sophisticated equipment,
    and larger vessels to carry more sitting Dene.

Unfortunately, the aging specialists faded away.
Some ships sailed without a captain, engineer, or stewardess.
Others remained anchored due to broken engines.
Their crew did a bit of caretaking,
    and kept encouraging the sitting Dene:

      "One day we'll show you how to run these ships.
      It will take time, everything is so complicated..."

The Dene sat and waited, until a Dene elder reflected:

      "I could still make a birchbark canoe."

Other Dene added:

> "We're still strong enough to paddle."

They left the big ships,
   and they invited the few remaining members
   of the Heavenward Company:

> "It will be kind of slow, sometimes pretty stormy too,
>   but if you like to come with us, you're welcome,
>   we will build canoes together,
>   we will all paddle,
>   we will all make it."

Bishop

People and nations in power always pretend
    that the world is as it should be.

When I was in elementary school, before World War II,
    my geography book showed nearly all of Africa
    painted red for the French colonies,
    and blue for the British colonies,
    'which was the way it should be.'

In Vendée, on the Atlantic coast,
    barons and viscounts surveyed the countryside
    from their castles on top of the hills.
Farmers bowed down to 'Our Master,'
    the land owner whose land they tilled,
    'which was the way it should be.'

In every little town,
    the mayor, the parish priest, and the police adjudant,
    'the civilian, religious, and military authorities,'
    worked hand in hand to protect 'the established order.'
Those local authorities were controlled
    by the district's 'prefect,' bishop, and general,
    'which was the way it should be.'

The bishop was closer to God than the other authorities.
What excitement, once every four years,
    when the bishop condescended
    to honor our small parish with his visit,
    in order to administer confirmation!

My brother Marcel was confirmed on May 10, 1939.
My mother, my younger brother and myself
    sat in church in our own places in our own pew
    (every family rented so much pew space yearly).

The bishop, wearing his mitre, solemnly entered the church,
    while the pipe organ blasted its loudest.
The mysterious personage ascended the main aisle
    while everyone in awe and admiration
    wondered if God walks in such a way in Heaven.

In the religious silence which followed,
    the bishop sat on his throne in the sanctuary.
My younger brother pulled my mother's sleeve,
    and in his clearest voice confided:

    "Mom, I like his carnival hat."

Confession

"Good afternoon, Father."

"Good afternoon, sir....My Gosh, is it you Larry?"

"Yeah, that's only me, but that's me."

"I haven't seen you for a year."

"It could well be, Father."
I was trapping in winter,
    prospecting in summer,
    way out in the bush.
Now, I want to go to confession."

"Why didn't you come earlier for confession?"

"I'm not sure, I was far away,
    and there's no highway over there."

"You could have come by dogteam in winter."

"Coming by dogteam would take weeks.
It's not worth such a long trip
    to confess only small venial sins."

"You could have chartered a plane."

"Father, planes are too risky
    if one has big mortal sins."

Dear Father in Heaven,

You must remember the time we were discussing
    whether or not I should become a man on earth.
I'm glad we went for it: my body's a marvel,
    and next month we'll celebrate my fifteenth birthday.

A few mornings ago, I woke up early, all was quiet,
    all I could hear was my heartbeat, so regular.
I wondered on what day my heart started to beat,
    and what keeps it going. It's life! But what is life?
I wish I could remember when I was a baby,
    when I walked my first steps, and fell for the first time.
What made me smile? What made me cry? Was I funny?

I'm telling you, it has been quite an experience
    having to learn everything through my senses,
    feeling hungry, thirsty, tired, sick, and sleepy,
    but also excited by love, grace, and beauty.

Heaven is O.K., but now I see with my own eyes
    soft ripples on the lake, magnificent Tabor,
    delicate butterflies, galloping horses,
    women drawing water, men leading their donkey.
I see children at play, I see my teenage friends:
    the boys growing up strong, and the girls so graceful.

I hear with my own ears thunder and sparrows' songs,
    my neighbours arguing or welcoming each other,
    faithful people repeating the words of your Covenant,
    Mary laughing her head off, and Joseph laughing at her.

Father, I love my hands which are strong and gentle.
I can use a hammer, saw a board with Joseph,
    shake hands, make a fist, and caress Myriam's face.

I enjoy our food: beans, lentils, salted fish,
    barley bread, wild honey, figs, olives, and red wine.

Spring flowers smell so sweet: red anemones, jasmine,
    saffron crocus, yellow laurels, and tamarisks.

It is great to be God, wonderful to be man.
    I cherish my body, and I celebrate you.

Your son, Jesus.

*A copy of this letter was discovered
by René Fumoleau in 1990.*

Dear Father in Heaven,

This coming Christmas will be my 30th birthday.

The highlight of the past year
    was my baptism by the ever popular John.
It is the opportune time to start my Church
    and to choose my Apostles.

I will select some Apostles
    from the seventy members of the Sanhedrin.
They have political power, make the laws,
    and can influence even the Romans.

First, I will pick up some of the Scribes.
I need jurists, writers, and Rabbi Masters.
I will even solicit Gamaliel,
    or one of those famous Doctors of the Law.

I want some of the strict observers of the Law,
    the well-respected Pharisees.
And at least one Zealot
    to attract the passionate militants into my Church.

Only one of the Sadduccees!
They resigned themselves to the Roman occupation,
    but they represent the aristocracy,
    the wealthy, and the Temple officials.

Should I try to approach Caiaphas, the High Priest?
He's kind of insignificant,
    but he's part of the High Nobility,
    and he's well considered by Pontius Pilate.

The Publicans collect taxes for Rome,
    and enrich themselves in this process;
I hope I can enlist at least two of them
    in order to finance my Church.

No more Galileans in my group!
Our accent is disgraceful to most Israelites.
Galileans are known as backward people
    and as lax observers of the Law.

I don't want any poor.
They have little to offer, and won't help our image.
When we are well organized,
    we'll be able to assist some of the worthy ones.

My Apostles will speak Hebrew, Aramaic,
    'and Latin, the language of the Empire.'
They will also learn Greek,
    the international business language.

My Apostles will learn to write
    on parchment, papyrus, and wax tablets.
I will design a seal
    to show the importance of all our correspondence.

Herod is a vassal of Rome,
    but, as tetrarch of Galilee, he has a lot of power.
I think it will take a few miracles
    before I get him to support my Church.

I wonder if I can use Pontius Pilate, the cruel Procurator.
He's in a bad spot:
He despises the Jews, but he's afraid of them.
He's still more afraid of Rome.

Where will I establish my headquarters?
Of course in Jerusalem, your Holy City.
I'll demand that some rooms in the Temple
    be reserved for my Church.

My Apostles and I will ride horses,
as the Roman soldiers do,
in order to impress the ordinary people
who usually travel on foot or with a donkey.

After each of their missions,
my Apostles will relax in modern residences
adorned with terraced gardens, fountains and swimming pools.

Father, you see how much planning I have done.
Within three years my Church should be a real success.

Merry Christmas to you.
Your beloved Son, Jesus.

A copy of this letter was discovered
by René Fumoleau in November 1989.

Christian Unity

Long before I arrived in Yellowknife in 1970,
    Indian trappers, Métis fishermen, White laborers,
    artists, prospectors, retired couples,
    people from twenty languages and nationalities:
    Kalmo, Slogget, Hudson, Broten, Desjarlais, Petrovitch,
    Kurz, Hedden, Beaulieu, Holms, Poole, Olson, Fredricson,
    had scattered more than sixty small houses
    between the unsurveyed roads of Willow Flats.
People were still free before the days of town planning,
    and they built houses to live in instead of for investment.

Each house had lived enough stories to fill up a volume,
    and conversations covered anything under the stars.
The language was as colourful as the tea was black,
    and for me every tale was a history lesson.

One cold winter afternoon,
    after many jokes and much laughter,
    Karl and his visitors turned serious:

        "René, I saw something in the newspaper
            about a week for Christian Unity.
        What's that?"

I tried to explain:

        "They say that Jesus Christ founded only one Church,
            but history, geography, cultures and languages
            divided it into many Churches.
        In Yellowknife alone there must be ten Christian
            Churches."

        "We must be really bad
        if it takes all those churches to save us."

"Or we must be really good
    if it takes all those churches to fit us in.
Whatever! For one week in February,
    all the churches try to pray and to work together
    in order to build more unity among themselves."

"Why do they have to pray for unity?
All those churches have always been united.
I hear all of them say the same creed:
'I believe in one God, the dollar almighty.' "

1903

I immigrated from France to Denendeh in Spring 1953.
Then, the Oblates went for vacation every ten years,
    and my father died in 1959, before I could see him again.
Later, regulations and travels became easier,
    and I visited my mother every three years
    until she died in 1978.

At every visit,
    her ears had become more lazy,
    and her eyesight more fuzzy.
She had never walked very fast
    because of a knee which didn't bend,
    but she was moving more slowly yet.
She filled her days with silence, prayer, knitting,
    and welcoming her grandchildren and friends.
She listened to 'good' radio programs,
    and was up to date on everything in the world:
    sports, music, education, politics.
Her mind was clear and her spirit bubbling.
She often shared with me her philosophy of history,
    and so, one day:

        "My little boy,
            in 1901, the government voted a law
            to restrict the organization and the work
            of the religious congregations in France.
        In 1902, Combes became Prime Minister,
            and he applied the new law with the utmost severity.
        Religious Brothers and Sisters were forbidden to teach,
            and 14,000 schools and religious institutions were closed.
        Most religious congregations were legally abolished.
        Thirty thousand of their members were banned.
            and escorted by the army to the borders of Switzerland,

Belgium, Spain, Italy, or Germany.
The government seized all churches, chapels,
    seminaries, rectories, and religious properties,
    including all deposits in retirement funds.
Later on, in July 1905, the National Assembly
    voted the Separation of Church and State.
Here, in Chantonnay, les Frères de Saint Gabriel
    who taught boys à l'Ecole Saint Joseph,
    were evicted in May 1903.
As you know, my parents, your grandparents,
    lived near l'Institution Sainte Marie,
    the school run by les Sœurs de la Sagesse.
In October 1903, I saw the soldiers
    pull the sisters out of the school,
    and march them to the railway station.
I followed them in the streets with my parents
    and a large crowd praying and singing hymns.
The whole parish was in distress:

      'Now, nobody will teach catechism to the children.'

      'Sisters and Brothers were such good educators.'

      'That's the end of religion, the end of the Church.'

We had been trained to obey all authorities,
    and nobody tried to stop the soldiers,
    or to rebel against the government.

I was nine years old at that time, and I wondered:
    'Will there be anybody to teach me now?',

and I was crying with everybody else."

I felt that my mom, reliving those wicked days,
    was ready to cry again.
Instead, she put her wrinkled hand on my wrist,
    and she bent a little closer as for a grand secret:

    "My little boy, there was so much pain in those days,
    ...but that's what saved the French Church."

Filipino Churches

Alliance Church,
Ambassadors for Christ,
Baptist Bible Church,
Bell Church,
Bethel Bible Institute,
Chi Alpha Christian Fellowship,
Christian Bible Church,
Christian Life Fellowship,
Church of Christ,
Church of the Nazarene,
Church of World Messianity,
Church on the Rock,
Cosmopolitan Church,
Day by Day Christians,
Episcopal Church,
Evangelical Church,
Faith Assembly of God,
First Church of Christ Scientist,
Foursquare Gospel Church,
Grace Bible Church,
Life Gospel Church,
Lord's Church,
Lutheran Church,
Memorial Christian Church,
Miracle Revival Church,
Missionary Fellowship,
New Testament Church of God,
Roman Catholic Church,
Seventh Day Adventists,
Star of Hope Church,
Union Church,
United Bethel Church,
United Church,
United Evangelical Church,
United Methodist Church,
United Pentecostal Church,

Wells of Salvation Christian Fellowship,
Wesleyan Church,
Word for the World Christian Fellowship,
Worldwide Church of God,
Youth for Christ.

Who said that the Third World
    is the playground
    of the First World's Churches?

Commitment

A group of Oblates discussing their commitments
were enthusiastic as well as cautious:

"As missionaries, we're in solidarity
    first of all with the Aboriginal people,
    but we have to be careful about consequences.
How far can we go? What if they make mistakes?
Should we approve and support everything they do?
Can we compromise our work with other people?
Their opponents may be our parishioners too."

Mary, an Aboriginal person herself, was present:

"Last year, when my daughter was about to give birth,
I wanted, I needed to be with her
    more than at any time during her twenty years.
I had raised her, I was proud of her,
    and nothing could stop me from being with her.

She had been in labour twelve hours already,
    and I was nearly as exhausted as she was.
I was waiting for the joyful miracle,
    when the doctor said she needed a cesarean.

I was not prepared and I started to panic:

      'No, not to my baby. I don't want it.
      It wasn't planned that way, it is not fair to me.
      I want to be with her but not to that point!'

I stamped my foot in anger, I rushed out of the room.
I walked three steps in the hallway...and I came back in."

Family

"Hi Donna. I haven't seen you since October,
   and it's already December 12."

"Freda, I can't believe 1988 is almost over.
How do you feel?

"In fact, I felt very good last night.
Did you see that T.V. program
   linking New York and Moscow teenagers?"

"Yes, they could see each other
   on giant screens in their own classroom."

"All of them chatted as old friends."

"Both groups sang in Russian and in English."

"They joked about the ups and downs of their own country."

"Young people communicate so easily!"

"They exclaimed across the miles:

   'You are cute!'

   'I love you,' 'I love you too.'

   'Thank you for the earrings.'

   'What music tape can I send you?' "

"I was moved when they sang together: 'The Tide is Turning.' "

"Me too, I was crying for joy."

"The program title 'Free to be a family' said it all."

"It's the best comment I've heard about Christmas so far."

"Do you know what the world really needs?"

"Maybe... I don't know..."

"Governments should be elected only by people under 19."

Inconvenience

In the Fall of 1990,
    the Innu of Nitassinan
    and the Alliance for Non-violent Action
    organized a 'Walk for Peace'
    from Halifax to Ottawa.
I joined them for one month,
    and we were welcomed everywhere,
    that is, except by one person, in La Pocatière:

    "I don't want to hear about Indians,
        about Indians from East or West,
        from any tribe or any reserve.
    I'm so fed up with Indians
        after the inconveniences
        they created for us this summer."

    "Sir, how were you inconvenienced here?"

    "Not us, but after the Indians
        barricaded the Mercier bridge,
        the White people from the south shore
        couldn't drive to Montreal.
    They had to use another bridge way upstream,
        an extra two hours drive."

    "How many people
        were inconvenienced?"

    "Could be four thousand."

    "And for how long?"

    "About two months."

"But sir,
    you know that in Canada
    four hundred thousand Indians
    have been very inconvenienced
    for over two hundred years."

"That's exactly what I mean!
Them Indians, they are used
    to be inconvenienced,
    but us, we are not."

Land Claims

Abe and Alice had been away for two months;
    they were anxious to see their home again.
But, nearing the front yard, they saw red.
Gone was the lawn they had manicured for years,
    replaced by potato plants.
What to do? uproot everything? or what?
How to find out who had stolen their yard?

They didn't have to wait for long.
A man walked through the front gate,
    uncoiled a hose, opened a faucet,
    and started to water the potatoes.

Abe and Alice rushed to him:

      "What the hell are you doing?"

      "I'm watering my potatoes."

      "What do you mean 'your potatoes'?
      This is our land."

      "These are my potatoes."

      "Who allowed you to plant them?"

      "Nobody had to. That land was useless,
      with nobody around, just like wilderness.
      I decided to develop it."

      "But you didn't ask for our permission."

      "You were not here."

      "But this is our land."

"If this is your land, you should be ashamed
     to have kept it useless for so long."

"But we lived here all our life.
This is my house and my land,
     given to me by my father,
     who got it from his father."

"But you didn't use it properly."

"I use it the way I want,
     and that's none of your business."

"But I'm using it in a better way.
That's progress."

"I have the right to have a lawn,
     and to relax in my lawn chair."

"You wasted a fertile land,
     but I, I worked hard to make it productive.
I paid for the seeds, I cared for those plants,
     and I'm going to harvest them when I want."

"Oh no! You are not! I'll take you to court.
I'm going to see the judge right now."

"That's your choice,
     but I promised one third of the crop to the judge."

Mice

"My dear brother and sister cats,
I have called you to this meeting
to ask you only one question:

Why do we want to kill all those mice?"

"Because they are too arrogant."

"Because they are too shy."

"Because they are too noisy."

"Because they are too quiet."

"Because they are too fast."

"Because they are too slow."

"Because they are too fat."

"Because they are too skinny."

"Because they are too ugly."

"Because they are too nice."

"Thank you all,
    I'm glad we all agree
        that we should kill them."

Needs

I left home
with my tent.

I got a few things,
and a one-room shack.

When I got a good job,
I needed a small house.

My work was so demanding,
I wanted a quiet backyard.

We married and got a mansion,
to impress our business friends.

We climbed to such high positions
that we moved to a wealthy district.

To exercise after the long office hours
we built a swimming pool and a tennis court.

Rapidly, we needed a cottage in the countryside,
two small cars, plus a fancier one for our holidays.

As we were so successful and had little time to rest,
we bought a beautiful old castle on a spacious acreage.

Our psychiatrist advised us that we needed more relaxation,
and we had to build a gymnasium, a stable, and a race track.

The bank we purchased added so much to our responsibilities,
that we needed a small plane to get away from it all at any time.

How can we ever meet
our increasing needs?

And what will we need
at the end of it all?

Engine

"Hi Matt, I knocked at your door, there was no answer,
    so I came around, and that's where you are."

"Yes, I've lived in that shed for days,
    repairing, overhauling my old car engine.
I rebored the cylinders, installed new rings,
    changed the carburetor, tuned it to perfection.
It couldn't sound any better. Listen to it."

"Wow! Congratulations!"

"Thank you. I know it's perfect."

"Your car will run so smoothly."

"No, I want to keep that engine here.
It sounds better when it runs by itself."

"So, what will you do with it?"

"I'll start it once in a while,
listen to it, enjoy its sound."

Beauty car

"Look at my car:

Full interior carpeting,
Reclining bucket seats,
Rear seat shoulder harness,

Dual remote mirrors,
Rear window defroster,
Side window demisters,

Bumper rub strips,
Counterbalanced hood,
Hatchback versatility,

Front and rear anti-sway bars,
Fog lamps, body-side cladding,
Styled wheels with trim rings,

Isn't my car a beauty?"

"Wow! It certainly is.
The engine must sound really good too.
Could you start it just for a minute?"

"I can't, there's no engine."

"There's no engine?"

"I don't need one.
My car looks good enough as it is."

My love

"My love,
don't you love
the fine clothes,
the expensive jewels,
the racing cars I bought for you?

My love,
don't you love
the trips I took you on,
the vacations I planned for you,
the select clubs I enrolled you in,
the magnificent house I built for you,
the receptions I organized to show you off?

My love,
don't you love
my friends,
my life style,
my gourmet cooking,
my elegant way of dressing,
my good taste about art and music?

My love,
don't you love
my high goals, my promotions,
my clever power games, my successful deals,
my vision of the world, my sensible decisions,
my wise political views, my religious convictions,
the wealth I accumulated, my generosity for the poor?

My love,
don't you love me?"

Old age pension

In the old days,
  most Dene never cared about their age:

  "It O.K. to be old if you are in good health.
  It's no fun to be young if you are sick."

But, when the Old Age Assistance Act was passed in 1951,
  everybody over sixty five jumped for joy.
Imagine! Getting forty dollars a month
  without doing any work for that money.
It had never happened before!

Three weeks after the first cheques arrived,
  a government agent visited Denínu Kúę́ (Fort Resolution).
Most old-timers welcomed him, but not Rosalie:

  "I didn't get my cheque."

  "Sorry madam, you are not sixty five years old."

  "Yes I am. Jimmy there he got a cheque.
  My mom told me I was that high when he was born."

  "Yes, our list shows that Jimmy is sixty five, but not you."

  "What about Mary Tie? She got her money.
  I was already a woman when she was born."

  "It cannot be, according to our records."

  "Go to the Mission and check when I was baptized."

  "We don't need any more records, we have our own."

"Maybe your records are not right.
Tim here he got his cheque,
    and, if he gets it, I should get it too."

"Let me check my list.
Yes, Tim is over sixty five, but not you."

"It just can't be."

"Oh yes madam, that's the way it is.
And I don't want to argue any more with you."

"I don't want to argue either, but Tim is my son."

Prayer

You did not proclaim solemn beliefs,
    preach with big words,
      or even give me sound advice.

You did not look taller than me,
    but you lay down on the ground,
      at my level, by my side, very close.

Your arm rested on my chest,
    on my heavy heart,
      as a lifting power.

Your breath caressed my cheek,
    as long as it took
      to quiet my own breathing.

What a prayer!

Second meeting of the Indian Brotherhood of the NWT, in Behchokǫ̀ (Rae) 1971, photo: Native Press.

*Norman Pierrot, Harvey Pierrot,
Ida Lennie, Wendy Lennie Radeli Kǫ́ę́
(Fort Good Hope) spring 1969.*

*Naedzo, of Dogrib descent, was recognized
as a prophet, and Dene from surrounding
communities came to him for advice. He died
in Délı̨ne , (Fort Franklin) in 1973, at the
age of 83, after being blind for many years.*

Published in "Denendeh" book, 1984. The first map published with Dene and English names.

Dehcho, between Łegǫhłı (Norman Wells) and Rádelı Kǫ́ę́
(Fort Good Hope), 1980, in Springtime.

Alfred Baillargeon and Noël Crapeau, Winter fishing,
Great Slave Lake near Tehetta (Dettah).

Rocky Mountains, 1976.

Dehcho River near Rádęłı Kǫ́ę́, 1984.

Dehcho, Mackenzie River,
in the Ramparts, near Rádelı Kǫ́ę́ (Fort Good Hope), 1979.
In the Fall, when the soil is saturated with rain water, the water drops from the
overhanging cliff, and partly freezes before reaching the shore.

Ptarmigan.
The only bird with the raven to remain in
Denendeh in winter; Ptarmigans are white in
winter, turn grey or brown in summer.

Photograph

The post office clerk handed me my parcel
    and my heart jumped:

    "I know what it is."

Full of expectation,
    I drove home through the October snowfall.

I stared at the 11" x 14" photo enlargement.
I held it closely, sideways, at arms' length,
    and finally I set it up against my cupboard.
The lab had printed it exactly as I wanted.

Three months previously, in July,
    at a coffee break during a meeting, Karen had told me:

        "I just moved to Yellowknife from Hamilton,
            and I love it so much up here,
            clean air, rugged scenery, lakes and rivers.
        I like hiking, I will ski, and I want to canoe."

        "I have a small 14-foot canoe.
        If you like to go canoeing one of these days..."

        "I would love to."

A week later, we drove to Prosperous Lake
    and paddled from Cassidy Point to Tartan Rapids.
We carried the canoe over the short portage,
    and watched the rapids from the safety of shore.
In this long summer day, we had ample time
    to paddle down the Yellowknife River to the bridge.
We canoed across the river below the rapids,
    and climbed the cliff overlooking Prosperous Lake.

We sat, talked, and nibbled a few apples.

The northeast breeze blew the mosquitoes away,
　　while a lonely eagle and flocks of gulls graced the sky.
The sunshine caressed the sail of a lone boat,
　　fast powercrafts trailed silver ribbons,
　　and water skiers carved strange designs on the water.

The Dene have taught me that every day,
　　every season, and every weather is beautiful.
They don't pass judgements like: "It's lousy...it's gorgeous,"
　　they simply state: "It's sunny... it's stormy... it's cloudy."
But, on top of that cliff, I still exclaimed:

　　"It's so beautiful!"

Karen joined me:

　　"Looks better than the best postcard I've ever seen."

I had my camera and I felt challenged:

　　"I'll take a photo that will look better than any postcard."

A few small trees nearby had grown at the right place.
The fluffy clouds were perfectly shaped.
Karen wore clothes of fresh colours.
But I was still fussy:

　　"I'll wait for the sailboat to glide further right.
　　And please, can you sit a bit more to the left?"

The enlargement I held in my hands three months later
　　proved that my photographic eye was still OK.

The following day,
　　with my framed photograph carefully wrapped up,
　　I rang Karen's door.

　　"René, I haven't seen you for two months.
　　Would you like a cup of coffee?"

"I would appreciate that.
And yourself how are you doing?"

"Marvelous! I made new friends,
    I like my work, I like my apartment,
    and the snow and the cold don't bother me."

She slowly opened my parcel, and her eyes sparkled.
She ran to the next room,
    and brought back a newspaper clipping:

    "Three days ago, the Edmonton Journal
    printed a photograph of my favorite singer."

She flipped my frame upside down,
    turned open the small clamps at the back,
    removed my photo,
    replaced it with her clipping,
    secured the backing,
    turned the frame right side up,
    and held it up proudly:

    "Look, the perfect frame for my clipping!"

Talents

(Matthew, chapter 25)

Jesus told his disciples:

"A rich man, going to travel for two or three years,
    entrusted his money to his servants:
    five million dollars to one,
    two million dollars to another,
    one million dollars to the third one.

The rich man returned, and asked for their accounts.

The first servant said:

'Sir, due to inside information,
    I made a killing at the stock market.
I bought old houses, chased the poor tenants out,
    tore the houses down, and I built luxury condominiums.
I got land very cheap from bankrupt farmers,
    and resold it at a 300% profit.
I invested your money in a foreign arms factory.
Your five million dollars grew into twenty million dollars.'

The second servant came up:

'Sir, I was tipped about horse racing,
    and I beat the odds at every horse track.
I made money at high-stake bingos and lotteries.
I gambled in Las Vegas, and I won and I won.
I started with your two million dollars,
I give you back five million dollars.'

The third servant brought back
    the one million dollars he had received:

'Sir, I helped refugees start a new life.
I helped needy folks to build low-cost housing.
I helped poor people to open a co-operative.
To all, I lent your money at no interest.
And I'm telling you, they were honest people,
    they repaid faithfully every dollar of their loans.
Here's your million dollars, right to the last cent.'

And the rich man declared:

'Well done, good and faithful servant,
    you can do great things with little money.
Come and join in your master's happiness.' "

Jennie

Hardly anybody knew his name,
    and most Dene called him 'that guy.'
Travelling down Dehcho from the South,
    he had landed at the village dock
    four days ago.

In that short time
    he had fallen in love with Jennie
    and he wanted to marry her.
Both were to fly out
    to morrow at 8:00 AM.

Jennie's parents listened to plenty of advice:

        "He seems to be rich."

        "He's but a smooth talker."

        "No! You shouldn't let her go."

        "Will he give you his boat?"

        "She's such a nice girl."

        "Same thing happened to Emma.
        She came back with nothing
            but the clothes she had on her back."

In the midst of their sadness,
Jennie's parents answered:

        "We have trained our daughter
            to be responsible for herself
            and to make her own decisions.
        This is her life.
        And if it doesn't work out,
            she'll know we still respect her,
            and she'll come back."

Yes, No

If my friend calls me,
I answer "yes,"
or "yes if," "yes but,"
"yes" but not quite,
"yes" but yes and no.

If my friend calls me,
I trust my friend
with my whole self,
or with only half of me,
with only my head,   .
or with only my heart.

My head wants to remain ahead,
to do what a head does best,
to control itself and everything.
My head ponders the cold facts,
but a flame burns my heart.

My head proclaims:
    "Here is my map, and my compass."
My heart sings:
    "Run swiftly, and get lost in love."

My head declares:
    "Be a solid rock."
My heart smiles:
    "Be waves and wind,
    sand and sun."

Head and heart pursue the dialogue:

"The waves may tumble you over."

"The rock may petrify you."

"You may spin endlessly in the wind."

"You may shrivel up on the rock."

"The sand is too loose and shifting."

"The rock is too immovable."

"There are limits and boundaries..."

"Over them the sun circles free."

Ts'ąkui Theda, 1990.

Ts'ąkui Theda

Ancestors of the present day Chipewyans
    built their log cabins at Desnedheché (Lockhart River)
    on the East Arm of Tunedhe (Great Slave Lake).
Trout and whitefish play in the clear water.
Blueberries ripen juicy on the river banks.

Most of the cabin roofs have collapsed,
    and the walls will slowly disappear
    in a circle of death and life:
Trees die, trees are born, the forest lives.

Every August, the Chipewyans from Lútsél k'é (Snowdrift)
    gather at Desnedheché in a week long pilgrimage
    to meet again their parents,
    grandparents, and great grandparents,
    to celebrate their achievements, their pains and loves,
    to celebrate the creation and the Creator,
    to celebrate themselves.

They come to visit Ts'ąkui Theda,
    the 'Old Lady Who Sits in the River,'
    who has been sitting for ten thousand years;
    or is it one hundred thousand years?

Ts'ąkui Theda is not a wooden or plaster statue.
She is living water and free Spirit.
She is one with the Eternal Power who loved her into existence.
She is the Goddess of the origin and of regeneration.

Her grandchildren extol her, and they value her care:

> "Every Fall since I was a child, long ago,
> > Ts'ąkui Theda kills a moose or a caribou for us.
>
> She lets it drift to the mouth of the river
> > just before we arrive at our camp.
>
> The meat is always fresh and it never spoils.
>
> She cures our sick, she makes us strong-minded people.
> We trust her, we humbly bring gifts to her.
> She shows her affection by showering mist on us,
> > and when I see the fog rising from her sacred place,
> > I know Ts'akui Theda is thinking of me."

(Maurice Lockhart, born 1911)

Most beautiful lady,
> spirit of the river, spirit of the Chipewyans,
> you bring kindness to a harsh land,
> you warm up the icy waters from the barren land.

In Summer, you exult with the heat of passion.
In Fall, you calm creation into rest.
In Winter, you sit serene in cold and darkness.
In Spring, you smile at the new life.

Mother Water alive with Mother Earth,
> you don't stand proud or arrogant,
> you don't lie down prostrated or defeated.
You sit secure for the future of the Chipewyans,
> protecting their land, river, and traditions.

Ts'ąkui Theda,
    wild and gentle,
    rigid and fluid,
    daring and timid,
    demanding and generous,

    you chill and excite me,
    you frighten and entice me,
    you grieve and comfort me,
    you captivate and liberate me.

Will you birth me into life?
Will you dance me into joy?

After their yearly pilgrimage,
    the Chipewyans leave their camp,
    and only footprints remain on the sand.

The boats steadily ride the waves.
The Chipewyans know where they come from
    through time.
They know where they are going
    through life.

Self-Government

For the 1991 Dene National Assembly at Bell Rock,
    campsites with water tanks and outdoor toilets
    were established for each of Denendeh's five regions.

Chiefs, councillors, delegates, and visitors
    had been gathering already for three days
    for serious discussions and joyful festivities.

On the fourth day, Saturday morning,

08:30. Joe goes to his band councillor:

> "A lot of Deh Gáh Got'įné (Slavey people) got here
>   yesterday evening.
> We need one more outdoor toilet in our camp."

08:42. Band councillor to his chief:

> "Joe said we need one more toilet."

08:51. Chief to the campsite maintenance worker:

> "My people need one more toilet."

08:59. Maintenance worker to supervisor:

> "They need one more toilet in the camp over there."

09:14. Supervisor, by radiophone, to contractor in Fort Smith:

> "Can you send someone to dig a toilet?"

09:16. Contractor to supervisor:

> "Sorry, it's Saturday, my crew doesn't work on
>   Saturdays."

09:21. Supervisor to maintenance worker

"There's nobody to dig a toilet today."

09:34. Maintenance worker to chief:

"Nobody to dig a toilet today."

09:41. Chief to councillor and to Joe:

"Cannot get another toilet today.
Can we manage with only one?"

09:43. Joe:

"Damn it. I'm so fed up with that administration.
I saw three shovels there, near the path.
I'll ask Clayton and Eddy to help me,
    and we're going to dig that damn shit hole.
There's a toilet lying down behind the bush there.
We'll bring it here and we'll set it up ourselves."

09:58 Joe, Clayton, and Eddy start digging.

10:42 The pit is dug, the toilet is up.

10:49 Joe looks at me:

"You've been laughing all the time since this morning.
Do you think it's funny?"

"No, I said, it's serious, very serious.
It's called self-government and self-determination."

Pater Pauperum

Hundreds of Dene and visitors took part
    in the 1980 Dene National Assembly
    in Rádełı Kǫ́ę́ (Fort Good Hope).

Our bishop showed up to celebrate the Sunday mass.
After the service, the chiefs and the bishop
    waited for the usual family photograph
    while people walked around and enjoyed themselves.

From the makeshift altar,
    still covered with liturgical vestments,
    Frank, a Dene, picked up a leather-bound missal:

        "What's that on the cover?"

        "It's the bishop's coat of arms."

        "What's that?"

My explanation seemed satisfactory to him,
    but he further inquired:

        "What's written under those arms?"

        "It's the bishop's motto."

        "What does it say?"

        " 'Pater Pauperum,' it's Latin,
        it means 'Father of the Poor.' "

Frank, unconcerned, dropped the book:

        "Who decides who is rich and who is poor?
        Besides, I don't know if we need a father,
            but we'd surely like to have a brother."

Muskeg Tea

In the Fall, a Dene family invited me
    to spend some time at their bush camp
    where they were preparing for the trapping season.
The log building was not luxurious but comfortable,
    because the ceiling had been insulated.

During my stay there, I never heard
    anybody giving an order to anybody else,
    or telling the children: "Do this." or "Don't do that."
While cooking, the mother would say:

      "There's not much water left in the barrel."

    which meant that somebody had to grab a pail
    and go down the river bank for water.

Or the father, without looking at the two boys:

      "We're running short of firewood."

The youngest child was about four.
She led her own life,
    wandering freely in and out of the house
    and in the bush nearby.
One afternoon, the little girl walked in,
    holding a few twigs of muskeg tea
    which she presented to her mother.
Muskeg tea, or Labrador tea,
    is a wild bush with narrow leaves.
It is prepared like regular tea,
or mixed with tea to add a special flavour.

It was the first time that the little girl
    contributed anything to the family.
The mother received the twigs with reverence,
    and she thanked her daughter,
    calmly, but with such joy and pride.
I felt privileged to witness
    the deep feelings flowing between mother and child.

The mother, holding the precious twigs,
    turned slightly towards me:

      "Tomorrow Sunday, you'll say mass with us?"

      "Yes."

      "I'm going to boil these leaves,
         and, instead of wine, we can use that tea for mass."

Mirror

Grandpa Anguway waited
   until we all sat comfortably around him:

    "Most Dene families led a solitary life.
    In Fall, we scattered all over our land,
       because the animals we depended on,
       they too, they scattered all over.
    We used to camp near a lake or a river,
       and our neighbours were
       fifty kilometres to the West,
       or one hundred to the North.

    Us, men and older boys,
       we hunted for moose or caribou.
    We visited our traplines by dogteam or on snowshoes,
       and each trip took a few days.
    The women remained at the camp,
       they raised the children,
       cut firewood, drew water from the lake,
       cooked, and washed the clothes.
    Summertime was easy time
    because we could travel by canoe.

    My grandfather, Matoway, told me that one year
       shortly after breakup, in June,
       his friend Tekay paddled to the trading post
       to sell a few beaver and muskrat pelts.
    On his way back Tekay noticed an old campsite,
       or rather a recent one,
       which he knew was not a Dene campsite.
    The way my grandfather was talking
       I guess it happened in the 1890s when prospectors
       drifted down Dehcho on their way to the Klondike.
    Until then, the Dene had never heard
       of white men looking for underground things.
    At that abandoned camp,
       Tekay picked up two nails, one empty tin can,
       and a small piece of glass which showed a human face.

He had seen drawings at the trading post,
    but nothing like that.

Back at his camp, Tekay emptied his babiche packsack:
    shells, sugar, tea, and tobacco.
His wife, Bella, picked up the piece of glass, and screamed:

    'Is that the pretty woman
        you went to see at the trading post?'

    'No, I never saw a woman there.'

    'Then, who drew up that face?'

    'I don't know, I found it on the river bank.'

Bella's mother, squatting on her heels
    at the back of the tent, inquired:

    'My daughter, why do you sound so upset?'

    'Mom, I think my husband
        visited that woman at the trading post.'

    'My daughter, show me that thing.'

The mother looked at the piece of glass,
    and she laughed so cheerfully that she cried.
Finally, she managed to address her daughter:

    'Why are you so disturbed?
    Which man would ever be interested
    in an old decrepit woman like her?' "

We loved Grandpa Anguway's rich voice,
    his brilliant eyes, his eloquent gestures,
    and he always promised:

    "That is only one story,
    I know many more stories."

Awards night

In April 1991, a few priests, religious brothers and sisters
    celebrated their jubilees in Sǫmbak'è (Yellowknife).
Each one received a standard congratulatory letter
    from Brian Mulroney, then Prime Minister of Canada.
The following night,
    a dream took me way far in space and way back in time.
I heard:

> "My dear friends,
>   Jesus' twelve Apostles
>   have successfully completed their second year of training,
>   and tonight they will receive their awards.
> I am your M.C. for this celebration,
>   and I want, first, to recognize our distinguished guest:
>   Herod Antipas, son of Herod the Great.
> As our tetrarch for the past 35 years,
>   Herod has provided employment for many of our friends.
> He has built a glorious city on the shore of the sea of Galilee,
>   and named it Tiberias after our emperor.
> No doubt the emperor will show his benevolence to our district
>   and to this small group of apostles
>   who do need a high ranking protector.
> Herod will now address you.
> Will you, please, stand up and acknowledge him?
> Thank you."

> "Dear apostles, this is Herod, your tetrarch, speaking.
> The Emperor, as a sign of his gratitude,
>   has sent to everyone of you a sheepskin parchment
>   wrapped in fine embroidered linen.
> I will read one of the twelve parchments,
>   the one addressed to Simon Peter:

> > 'Greetings from your Emperor!
> >   With great joy I learned
> >   that you cure sick people, raise the dead,
> >   and feed multitudes with only a few loaves.

Thank you for backing up our relief programs
    and for building healthier citizens for the Empire.
Thank you for reminding all my subjects
    to pay their taxes scrupulously,
    and to give to me, Caesar, what belongs to me.
Work along with my friend Herod
    to bring order and prosperity to your district.
I, your Emperor, and the Gods will protect you.'

My dear friends,
The twelve parchments are signed: Your beloved Emperor.
Now, let us stand and sing: 'Gods save our gracious Emperor!'

Unfortunately, I woke up before the singing started.

Chocolate

In August 1992, in France,
   I bought a 'Toblerone' chocolate bar,
   the kind worth 85 cents in Canada.

On the wrapper I read the description:

   –Zwitserse Melkchocolade met honing-en amandel-nougat.

   –Schweizer milchschokolade mit honig-und mandel-nougat.

   –Chocolate suizo con leche extrafino y nougat de miel y almendras.

   –Chocolate de leite com nougat de mel e amendoas.

   –Swiss milk chocolate with honey and almond nougat.

   –Chocolat au lait suisse avec nougat au miel et aux amandes.

   –Cioccolato svizzero al latte con torrone al miele e mandorle.

   Europeans can live
      with seven languages on a chocolate bar.

   Canadians fight wars
      when both English and French
      are printed on a box of corn flakes.

Conformity

Springtime! I sit in the bush.
The East wind is still cold,
    but new leaves timidly appear.
Trees surround me, all spruce trees,
    except one solitary birch tree,
    the only birch tree as far as I can see.
Should I cut it down for the sake of conformity?

Last day of May! I stand on the lake shore.
Seventy five seagulls are crowded
    on the last ice floe on Back Bay.
Among them one raven, only one black raven.
Should I shoot it dead for the sake of conformity?

Fall! No more mosquitoes! I lie on the ground.
All the birchtrees have turned yellow.
But near me, one birchtree remains green.
Only one green birch tree.
Should I cut it down for the sake of conformity?

November !
All snowflakes are white.
Conformity, finally!

Click!

The Oblates arrived in Canada in 1841.
To celebrate this 150th. anniversary,
    our Oblate province published a book
    with photographs of all its members.
Every Oblate had his photo taken
    during the annual retreat in February.
'For uniformity,' everyone was required
'to wear a roman collar or a tie.'

Karsh photographed Helen Keller, Albert Einstein,
    Martha Graham, Pablo Casals, Marian Anderson, etc...
His portraits reached the soul
    and the uniqueness of each person.

Every Oblate also has a unique life,
    and has been timely photographed
    praying in church or listening to music,
    smoking his pipe or teaching children,
    building a house or welding a boiler,
    driving a truck or loading a barge,
    enjoying a picnic or leading a workshop,
    repairing shoes or cooking for twenty,
    fixing his car or paddling his canoe,
    laughing and joking or tearful and in pain.

But the authority wanted photographs of uniform Oblates.
So, everyone had to sit on the same chair,
    with the same neutral background,
    and under the same flash.
Each had to turn his shoulders this way,
    tilt his head slightly the other way,
    and hopefully smile a uniform smile.

So it happened that Felix told me:

        "It's your turn to be photographed.
        Do you have a roman collar?"

"Not for at least 25 years."

"Do you have a tie?"

"Not since 1945."

"Do you like to borrow my tie?"

"Sure."

So, the photographer was the only person
to see me with a tie in 45 years.

Click ! I became a uniform Oblate!

In the army I was number 10767.
My uniform was more important than me,
and any corporal had the right to destroy me.
I was totally powerless then,
but why, 40 years later,
did I accept such manipulation?

For years, I have been proclaiming
people's right to self-determination,
and the right of all to make decisions for themselves.
But I didn't have the healthy reaction to say:

'Forget the collar or tie photograph.'

Why did I put on a tie?
Why do people accept being enslaved?

'It's no use to rock the boat.'
'Well, it's not worth making a fuss.'
'If they want it that way, let's do it.'
'If that makes them happy, might as well.'
'It's only a small detail, so what?'

No, there is no small detail in a degrading process.
Someone said two thousand years ago:

'Whoever is not faithful in small matters
will not be faithful in large ones.'

Did I hate myself and my photograph?
Did I learn from my mistake?
Questions for anyone who accepts playing games.

Experience

Jack showed me his shelves with pride:

"Look at my books:

>   'Awareness'
>   'Discovery'
>   'Experience'
>   'Self-knowledge'
>   'Do it yourself'
>   'Be your own teacher'
>   'Learn from your own'
>   'Growing into yourself.'

René, they're great books. They taught me
    that experience is the best teacher,
    that one cannot learn from reading,
    but only from trying and experimenting.
I love those books,
I read them over and over again.
I want to buy more of that kind of book."

*   *   *

Dale and Shelly, new-comers to Denendeh, visited me:

>   "René, we came to learn from you,
>   because you learned
>   not from other people,
>   but from your own experience.
>   That's why we want to learn from you!"

Counseling

"Good morning, Father."

"Good morning, sir."

"I am new here, and I thought that you..."

"If you're begging, you came to the wrong place.
 I've seen too many already."

"No, I am not begging, but as you are a priest..."

"Are you Catholic?"

"It could be."

"Have you been baptized?"

"I think so."

"Were your parents Catholics?"

"Oh yes."

"Are you married? I mean in the Church?"

"My wife died years ago.
I raised our two children myself
    until they could manage on their own."

"Do you want to go to confession?"

"I don't think so."

"Do you go to mass on Sundays?"

"Sometimes. I pray here and there."

"Could you help in our parish organizations?"

"I don't know what it means, so probably not."

"You don't expect anything from the Church.
On the other hand, you cannot help us.
Then, why did you come here?"

"I am looking for someone, a kind of counselor
to help me in my spiritual life.
So I thought that you..."

"Well, if you came for that..."

Michael

On an island in the middle of Great Slave Lake
    where raging summer storms and winter gales run free
    a solitary tree stands as a skeleton.
Its trunk, crooked and twisted as a corkscrew,
    is not worth even to be cut for firewood.
That tree has done the best it can to live and grow.

On Vancouver Island, I saw a cedar tree
    which is hundreds upon hundreds of years old.
In fact, I never saw its top, lost in the clouds.
To circle its trunk I walked more than twelve steps.
That tree has done the best it can to live and grow.

On top of the Latham Island cliff, I knelt down
    to see a birch tree born in the crack of a rock.
Probably ten years old, it's not ten inches tall.
That tree has done the best it can to live and grow.

In the rich silty soil along the Slave River
    millions of spruce trees rise in freedom and majesty.
Those trees have done the best they can to live and grow.

Near Great Slave Lake, a young tree was growing up strong,
    and we witnessed his branches spreading, beautiful,
    until winter lightning struck him down.
That tree did the best he could to live and grow.

Wait

Wait! you're not ready to be born.
   You don't know how to breathe with your lungs.

Wait! Keep lying down.
   You never practiced how to stand up, walk, or run.

Wait! Keep silent.
   You never learned how to speak.

Wait! Don't go into the water
   unless you can swim.

Wait! Don't go to school.
   You don't know what schools are all about.

Wait! Never buy anything by yourself
   if you haven't learned how to shop properly.

Wait! Don't ride a bicycle.
   until you learn how to keep your balance.

Wait! Don't do any work
   before you get used to it.

Wait! Don't get married.
   You don't know a thing about marriage.

Wait! Don't have any children yet.
   You have no experience about raising them.

Wait! Don't get old.
   You don't know what old age means.

Wait! Don't die.
   You have never done it before.

Dene life

Southern tourists visiting Sahtú (Great Bear Lake)
and Délı̨ne (Fort Franklin)
were ecstatic about the scenery
and about the Dene way of life:

> "Open sky,
> pure air,
> immense lake,
> gentle breeze,
> endless summer days.
>
> Clear water,
> delicious fish,
> game in the bush,
> wild ducks and geese,
> firewood everywhere.
>
> Sharing habits,
> elders' wisdom,
> carefree children,
> friendliness towards all,
> working only when you like,
> or when you decide you have to.
>
> Freedom from enslaving gadgets,
> and from keeping up with the Jones.
> Freedom from worrying about timers,
> laws, fences, regulations,
> gang wars, organized crime,
> traffic jams, hour-long commuting,
> mortgages, interest rates, and political games.

Do you appreciate your freedom?"

"Yes, we do."

"But, you Dene don't seem to feel enthusiastic
about all that you have?"

"I guess we are,
but we never had anything worse
to compare it with."

Carmelita

Carmelita wears a white towel over her head,
    a T-shirt with a faded message,
    a long blue skirt, and cheap sandals.
In the midst of Manila heat, noise, and pollution,
    she sits on the sidewalk of Aurora Boulevard,
    behind a small box full of treasures:
    chewing gum, mint candies, and cigarettes
    which are sold one at a time
    for half a Peso (about two Canadian cents).
Lucena, Carmelita's six-year old daughter,
    sits nearby, attending her personal 'Survival School.'

Dozens of equally enterprising peddlers
    offer comics, peanuts, sunglasses, newspapers,
    clothespins, jewelry, and other necessities.
Thousands of people walk by Carmelita every day,
    and, when business is brisk, she may earn five Pesos.
What's that when the cheapest rice costs nine Pesos a kilo?

Every evening, long after the 6 P.M. sunset,
    Carmelita and Lucena walk back home,
    about thirty minutes northward on the Boulevard.

Their home, built on the sidewalk,
    is four metres long, and two metres wide.
The walls are constructed of
    a few cement blocks, a rusty iron gate,
    five pieces of plywood which used to be pink,
    and a large sign still advertising 'Pepsi.'
When the blanket replacing the door is pulled up,
    a piece of white linoleum shines clean and bright.
The roof is an assembly of cardboard, plastic,
    and 'G.I.,' which, in the Philippines, means: galvanized iron.
The breeze blows freely through the house,
    and also the noise and the dust from the heavy traffic.

Three stones supporting an aluminum kettle
    are called the family kitchen, behind the house,
    in the ruins of a warehouse now littered with garbage.

When Carmelita got home, on the evening of March 12,
    her older boy told her: "The baby is sick."
Yes, she was sick, yes, she breathed with difficulty,
    but clinics, nurses, medicines, and hospitals
    were luxuries way out of reach.
The baby drank a spoonful of a brownish 'magic' liquid,
    and everyone fell asleep from exhaustion.

It was still dark when Carmelita woke up,
    lit the candle, and looked at the baby.
She screamed faintly,
    covered her mouth with one hand,
    and her eyes with the other.
Three fingers were missing on the baby's right hand.
There had been no cry.
The rats knew before the mother that the baby was dead.

Children's Rights

On May 5, 1989,
    a TV program celebrated the 30th anniversary
    of the Declaration on Children's Rights,
    mostly by showing violations of those rights:

    starving children in Ethiopia,

    children mentally disturbed for life,

    young male and female prostitutes in Thailand,

    children abandoned, orphaned, or maimed by bombs
        in the streets of Beirut and in other wars,

    Black children who are but statistics in South Africa.

The TV program didn't show the tragic situation
    of First World children who are taught:

    "Exploit the Third World to enrich your own country."

    "Get rich by selling arms which feed wars over there."

    "Satisfy your cravings even if you create starvation in Ethiopia."

    "Enjoy your parents' excessive power
        even if it is linked to prostitution in Thailand."

    "Build yourself a mansion even if it prevents
        one hundred families elsewhere from having simple shelters."

    "Enjoy your privileges,
        even if they rob others of their rights."

    "Do whatever profits you,
        regardless of the consequences for others."

"Get to the top of the ladder,
        whatever the number of people you must push down."

Deprived children
    raised in egoism,
    uneducated in humanity.
    illiterate in compassion.
    misinformed of the Divine Mystery.
    blind to the interdependence of all living beings.

Don't 'Children Rights' include a right to the truth?

Oranges

In the early 1950s, in Rádeli̧ Kǫ́ę́ (Fort Good Hope),
    air transportation was a luxury.
Twice a week, a DC-3 flew from Edmonton
    to Łegǫhłı (Norman Wells),
    and, if no mechanical problems developed,
    it returned to Edmonton the next day.

The town of Inuvik wasn't born yet.
From Łegǫhłı (Norman Wells), one Norseman plane served
    Tulít'a (Fort Norman), Délı̨ne (Fort Franklin),
    Rádeli̧ Kǫ́ę́ (Fort Good Hope),
    Tsı̨gehtshık (Arctic Red River), Teetl'ı̨t Zheh (Fort McPherson),
    Aklavik, and Tuktoyaktuk.
'Pappy' Hill was the pilot, the safest one in the world,
    who didn't need the Department of Transport's regulations.

Airports were not even in the planning stage,
    and the Norseman, on skis in winter, on floats in summer,
    'landed' on Dehcho, Mackenzie River.
Each Fall during freeze-up, and each Spring during break-up,
    the plane couldn't reach us for a few weeks.

The main summer attraction
    was the arrival of the boats and barges.
The first boat in June, was Streeper's.
It travelled down the Naechagáh (Liard River)
    from Fort Nelson to Łíídlı̧ Kǫ́ę́ (Fort Simpson),
    and down Dehcho to the Arctic coast.
One Spring, it had carried bananas,
    which spoiled before reaching the first port of call.
Even if that one experiment was not repeated,
    we still called it the 'Banana Boat.'

The Hudson's Bay Co., the R.C. Mission,
    McInnis Co., and the Yellowknife Transportation Co.
    operated boats and barges over the northern waters.
By far, the main fleet was the N.T.C.L.,
    the Northern Transportation Company.

All the supplies needed for one year,
    food, clothing, furniture, and building material,

travelled on the 'Muskeg Express' train
    from Edmonton to Fort McMurray.
Thence boats and barges
    plied the Athabasca and the Desnedhé (Slave) rivers
    to Tthebatthıé (Fort Fitzgerald).
Thence, the freight was trucked to Tthebacha (Fort Smith)
    over the twenty five-kilometre portage road.
From Tthebacha, boats and barges
    sailed down the Desnedhé river to Tucho (Great Slave Lake)
    and down Dehcho to the Arctic coast.

In Rádelı Kóé, the freight was unloaded
    at the southern end of the village, at the 'The Point'
    where small Jackfish Creek meets mighty Dehcho.
Forklifts hadn't found their way North yet,
    and the Dene, for one dollar an hour,
    carried the freight ashore on their shoulders
    and rolled the 45-gallon gas and oil drums up the steep bank.
What a scene when it rained and the mud was ankle deep!

We had not tasted eggs, apples, oranges, and fresh produce
    since the last boat of the previous summer, in September,
    and the fifteen White people living in Rádelı Kóé
    waited impatiently for the fresh eggs
    which had left Edmonton four weeks earlier.

Dene men and women were rather dreaming
    of the C.O.D. goods ordered months earlier
    from the Eaton's and Simpsons Sears' catalogues.

Every Spring, the Hudson's Bay manager
    opened the first box of oranges
    and gave one to the children present on the shore,
    that is every child in the village.

The children held their oranges in their hands,
    looked at it, squeezed it slightly,
    caressed it, turned it around and around,
    showed it to each other, and smiled
    while their eyes questioned:

        "Will you treasure yours a bit longer?"

        "Will you be the first one to peel it off?"

Marie and Charles

In 1670, the British Crown granted to the Hudson's Bay Company
    some trading rights over the northern part of America.
Those 'rights' were relinquished in 1870,
    and the British Crown transferred its northern domain
    to the three-year-old Canada.
Both transactions overlooked the rights of the Aboriginal Nations
    which had occupied and used that land for thousands of years.

The Canadian government,
    unconcerned about how the Aboriginal Nations called their land,
    named it the Northwest Territories.
Colonial powers relate to everything from their own location
    which they consider to be the centre of the world.

In 1970, the Northwest Territories' centennial year,
    Queen Elizabeth, Prince Philip, Prince Charles, and Princess Anne
    visited Frobisher Bay, Inuvik, Fort Smith, and Yellowknife.

In Yellowknife, on July 8, from 8:30 to 10:30 P.M.,
    a formal dinner gathered the Queen and the Prince,
    Jean Chrétien, then Minister of Indian Affairs, and his wife,
    and everybody who was somebody in Yellowknife.

To ensure that all bodies who were nobodies
    could somehow join in that day's celebrations,
    a barbecue was organized from 9:15 to 10:35 P.M.,
    at popular McNiven beach, then not yet polluted.
Hundreds of people converged at the beach
    to have a glimpse at Prince Charles and Princess Anne,
    and to dine on free hamburgers and corn on the cob.

As I stood on the beach, munching my corn
    and talking with Marie Bayamon,
    I noticed Prince Charles walking towards us.

A short distance behind him,
    three bodyguards in plain cloth
    blended well with the rest of the crowd.
Yellowknife wasn't yet modern enough
    to need tight security measures.

I stepped a few feet aside,
    and Charles and Marie faced each other:

    "Good evening, madam, where are you from?"

    "I'm from Yellowknife."

    "How long have you been here?"

    "I've been here all my life.
    I am a Dene, I was born here."

Marie pointed her cob at the prince:

    "And you, what's your name?"

    "My name is Charles."

    "Where are you from?"

    "I am from London, madam."

    "You mean London England?"

    "Yes madam, London England."

    "How did you get here?"

    "I flew from London to Montreal,
        thence to Frobisher Bay and to Yellowknife."

    "Are you going to stay here?"

    "No madam, only for three days."

    "Where will you go from here?"

    "I will go back to London."

    "How will you go back?"

    "I will fly from here to Edmonton and to London."

    "You're going to fly again, all the way back?"

    "Yes madam."

    "Gee! You must be rich!"

Cookie and Goldie

The real name of Fort Franklin is Délįne,
    the village near 'the fast water which never freezes.'
In 1960, two hundred and fifty Dene lived there
    under the guidance of their chief, councillors,
    and the occasional general assemblies.
The White population comprised the store manager and his clerk,
    two or three teachers, and myself as priest.
Somehow, we managed to live well without scheduled flights,
    mail and phone service, radio and T.V. reception,
    and without R.C.M.P., administrator, or government official.

Tulít'a, Fort Norman, lay sixty airmiles to the west,
    or ninety miles by Sahtú Dé, the Bear River.
Tulít'a looked like an important center
    with two R.C.M.P., one Indian Agent, and two nurses:
One was Cookie, close enough to her family name Cooke,
    the other one was Goldie, her first name.
In turn, they visited Délįne but much too seldom,
    because we all appreciated their services.

We cleaned and remodeled 'the' small yellow shack,
    and furnished it with a stove, a bed, chairs, pots and pans,
    so the nurses could come more often and stay longer.
William, the school janitor, ran a most primitive power line
    from the five-kilowatt generator to the nurses' shack.

In 1964, communications improved greatly.
The Forestry Services wanted all forest fires reported,
    and it supplied each Dene village with a two-way radio set.
Délįne people agreed that, whenever a nurse was present,
    she should be in charge of the radio set.
It could be useful also for medical emergencies.

Whenever a nurse was present in Délµne,
   she regularly discussed health situations,
   and chatted a bit, with her friend in Tulít'a.
One afternoon, the store manager and myself
   were visiting and drinking tea with Goldie.
Punctually at 2 P.M., she called Cookie,
   and she talked, and talked, ... until the electricity went off,
   which was common with the old generator.

Goldie, not a person to give up, carried on:

   "Cookie, the power is off, I know you cannot hear me,
   but I still have a message for you. Don't turn your set off.
   I'll send my message as soon as the power comes back.
   It's important, wait a while, and keep your set on."

SAD

"Good morning, Mrs. Eklakak."

"Good morning."

"Do you have SAD?"

"I don't know if we have any.
I'll ask my old man."

"No, I mean, are you a SAD case?"

"Yes, I am sad sometimes."

"I don't mean sadness.
Do you have Seasonal Affective Disorder?"

"You think my house is not in order?"

"No, your house is fine.
I'm a psychiatrist from Alberta Hospital,
    and I'm doing some research on SAD."

"Excuse me. You don't speak English as we do.
I'll call my daughter, she was in school."

"Good morning, Miss Eklakak.
As I was telling your mother,
    Seasonal Affective Disorder
    is one of the quirkiest illnesses,
    which even to me is still largely a mystery."

"No, I've never got that, I had T.B., mumps,
    scarlet fever, stomach flu, but not that kind."

"You must suffer from SAD.
In Florida, 1.4% of people suffer from SAD,
    in New Hampshire 8%, in Edmonton, 12%.

Consequently, near the Arctic Ocean,
    where there's no sun for more than a month,
    at least 18 % of people must suffer from SAD,
    and I am doing a survey to prove it.
Are you aware that the lack of light in winter
    makes animals slow down, or even hibernate?"

"My parents told me about the animals.
My grandparents too, they said
    it was like that way before their time,
    may be even for ever."

"And I want to prove that the lack of light
affects people as well as animals."

"Of course, that's the way it should be."

"Do you sleep longer in winter than in summer?"

"It has always been like that."

"I met a woman who came from Sarnia to Inuvik six weeks ago.
She feels very distraught, she often sleeps in,
    she feels she is in hibernation,
    and that's a horrible feeling."

"Why is it horrible? It's OK to slow down.
It's OK to sleep more in winter."

"She said she has to drink a lot of coffee to stay up,
    but even that, she keeps falling asleep."

"It's OK to fall asleep when you feel like it."

"From what you tell me I can surmise
    that you have SAD but you are not aware of it.
Luckily there is a treatment for you.
You need to be exposed to full-spectrum light."

"Spectacles? No, my eyes are OK."

"I mean, full-spectrum light
    is like a man-made version of sunlight.
The light travels through your eyes to the pineal gland
    and suppresses the production of malatonin,
    the hormone affecting the body's mood and sleep patterns."

"I guess I'll wait. The sunlight will come back at the right time."

"But in the meantime, you need to wear
    one of those newly developed light visors.
It costs only 349 dollars, that's U.S. dollars, plus GST.
The treatment was pioneered by Dr. Alfred Lewy
    at the U.S. National Institute of Mental Health."

"They have no light in the U.S. too?"

"My dear, they invented the visors not for themselves
    but for you unfortunate people living in darkness."

"My brother wore something like that on Halloween night."

"Miss, this is no fun. We are discussing a serious illness."

"All the Inuit must have had that illness
every winter for thousands of years."

"But they didn't know it.
Now that you know it, you have to treat it."

"My parents always say it was easier in the old days."

"Do you like summer with its 24-hour sunlight?"

"Summer is a good time too. I like it as much as winter."

"But in summer time, do you suffer from hypomania,
    the inability to slow down.?"

"We do a lot of things in summer,
    that's the time to do a lot of things."

"I've got no further question, Miss.
        People like you really spoil my survey."

Insults

In the good old days, before the snowmobile era,
    dogs outnumbered people in every Dene village.
Hours upon hours of conversation
    related to dogs, dogteams, and leaders (lead dogs).
No fish story could ever compare with dog stories.

Every man knew everyone else's dogs
    besides his own who were, of course,
    the fastest and the most resistant.
Leaders were the aristocracy of the dog society.
They also saved many people's lives:
    a good leader could cross a lake through miles of fog,
    or a frozen muskeg where the wind had erased all signs.

In Délı̨ne, Fort Franklin,
    Jimmy's dogs were hauling a heavy load of firewood
    on the trail between the mission building and the lake.
Suddenly the leader turned to the left
    and Jimmy coaxed him with a vibrant: "Huh."
The dog obeyed for five steps, and veered left again.
Jimmy walked to the leader, set him in the right direction,
    and all went well... for five more steps.
The 'huhs' became angry and forceful,
    but the leader had plugged his ears for good.

The problem, when one was mad at dogs,
    was that Dene languages had no swear words.
Jimmy's choicest Dene words didn't impress the leader.
Fortunately, people learning a second language
    usually start with the swear words,
    and Jimmy could revert to English:

"You devil of a stupid dog!

You dirty bag of useless lazy bones!

You no brain idiot no good for nothing!"

Jimmy was rapidly out of breath, and out of scornful words,
but he regained his lung power to launch the supreme insult:

"You, son of a bitch!"

Mother

As a young Dene,
   Kinlo had left home
   for a small town, and a big city,
   and a correctional centre,
   and a jail, and a penitentiary.

Fifteen years later,
   he was on his way home and he wondered:

   "My relatives, my friends,
       will they look at me, or turn their back?
   My mom, will she rejoice, or cry, or both?
       will she scold me for those wasted years,
       and for all the care I didn't provide?"

The Cessna landed on the gravel airstrip.
Kinlo shook hands with a few people,
   and glanced at many children he didn't know.

His mother was sitting
   in the home he had almost forgotten.
Mother and son sat silently for a while.
How does one start? who will start?

Her eyes calmly reached up for his:

   "Son, can you get the basin over there,
       and bring me a bit of warm water
       to wash my hair?"

Up

"I've been watching you for days.
Sometimes you must be cold,
    worried, and frustrated,
    not knowing what will happen.
Must be dangerous too."

"Any trade has its ups and downs.
Dreams come true, dreams crash down.
Usually, I make enough money
    to feed myself and my child,
    and to pay the monthly rent."

"If you come to my house sometimes,
I'll prepare good food for you.
You need to fill yourself up
    and to improve your health.
I'll get you pretty clothes and fancy shoes,
    a bit of silk, something chic, and real jewels.
I have the kind of makeup you need.
I'll call my hairdresser, she's a wonder.
Then, you won't be a prostitute any more.
You'll be a real call girl."

Mountains

"Mountains,

caressed by the soft sunrise,
scorched by the fiery sun,
adorned by the red sunset,

slapped by ferocious winds,
scrubbed by torrential rains,
stricken by frantic lighting,

prudishly covered with snow,
timidly hiding behind the fog,
childishly playing in the clouds,

crowned with glory,
resplendent with light,
decorated with spring flowers,

what do you do to be so beautiful?"

"Nothing special,
    we are mountains,
    we are simply what we should be."

NATO

"Dear Innu people of Labrador,
We, the N.A.T.O. airforces,
we are sorry that our training flights over your country
destroy your land, your animals, and your way of life.

But such training flights are necessary
so that, in the future,
we can prevent enemy planes from flying over your country
to destroy your land, your animals, and your way of life."

Embers

I wake up at 5:30.
The outside thermometer reads minus 25, usual for March.
Plus 15 inside, usual in the morning.

I finger the wood stove: Not cold, not warm either.
I turn and open the damper
    in case smoke still lingers in the fire box.

I kneel and I open the stove door.
I lift up a small, lifeless, blackened piece of wood,
    but underneath hides a tiny red ember.

So tiny that the smallest draft could blow it away.
I gently caress it with my breath,
    it grows somewhat redder, but no flame.

On the ember I carefully place
    three wood slivers, as small as matches.

I blow slowly. A timid flame springs up.

I blow slowly.
The original ember burns out
    but part of one sliver turns reddish.

I blow slowly,
    pausing between one breath and the next.
A tiny flame dances.

Mindful not to crush life,
    I deposit a sliver the size of my small finger,

I blow slowly. A clear flame leaps.
A whisper of smoke glides up.

A larger stick, denser smoke, more crackling.

O life!

1975–1995

1975

"René,
You crisscross Canada promoting your book.
You go to Dettah for the church services.
You attend too many meetings.
You lecture in too many places.
You spend too much time on correspondence.
You give too many radio and television interviews.

Why don't you slow down?
You spread yourself too thin.
You need time for rest, prayer, and silence."

1976
1977
1978
1979
1980
1981
1982
1983
1984
1985
1986
1987
1988
1989
1990
1991
1992
1993
1994

1995

"René,
Why don't you get more involved.
You could still organize many things?
You could serve two or three parishes.
You could perform all kinds of ministries.

Why do you want to retire?
What will you do? Just rest and pray?

Some priests still work at 84,
    and you're only 69!"